Fir for Luck

Barbara Henderson

pokey
hat

First published in 2016 by Pokey Hat

Pokey Hat is an imprint of Cranachan Publishing Limited

ISBN: 978-1-911279-09-9

eISBN: 978-1-911279-10-5

Cover photographs © shutterstock.com

©KatarzynaSieradz ©Aleshyn_Andrei ©olshole
and © Can Stock Photo Inc. / Miramiska

Illustration of Cooking Pot ©Nicola Poole used with permission of Nicola Poole

www.cranachanpublishing.co.uk

@cranachanbooks

cranachan

'Steeped in atmosphere, tension and the lyric cadences of the Highlands, Janet's tale lights a fire of courage and hope in a shameful and tragic period of Scotland's past. Henderson's debut is brave and beautiful.'

Elizabeth Wein

Author of *Code Name Verity* and *Rose Under Fire*

Cooking Pot

Illustration by Nicola Poole

A typical 1840s longhouse interior, showing the central hearth, cooking pot and chain

For

Carla: Spirited, creative, sparky.

Isla: Thoughtful, loyal, endlessly supportive.

Duncan: Enthusiast. Excited about any story - ever.

and **Rob**: Soulmate. No more said.

Contents

CHAPTER ONE

Strathnaver, 1814: The Inferno

'THEY'RE GOING TO BEGIN FURTHER DOWN THE HILL.' Anna's breaths came fast now, but nothing prepared her for what she was to witness next.

The first rider didn't greet the tenant. He didn't dismount, or reason, or plead, or argue. He looked at Sellar. And Sellar gave the smallest hint of a nod.

The rider hurled his torch at the dry thatch of the house. Within seconds, the roof was ablaze.

Anna's brain whirled. John leant against the wall for support—the home he had built with his own hands. Scenes of horror continued to play out in the valley: children and an old man were now stumbling from the burning building, stooped with the effort to breathe.

They watched as distant neighbours ran to retrieve what they could, twice, three times, and then no more as the burning roof collapsed inwards. Furious flames licked the *grey stones charcoal-black.*

'Help me, John!' Anna suddenly shouted. 'Help me; HELP ME!'

Wee Johnnie played among the bracken while his desperate parents pulled out chests and box beds and dresser and cloth, stacking it all against the rock face a little way off. More and more houses went the way of the first, and the sky darkened with the putrid smell of hell.

The inferno.

CHAPTER TWO

Ceannabeinne: 1841

'But Granna...'

'No!'

I groan and watch the curls of peaty smoke dance their way through the thatch above. Granna's face flickers in the dim light of our longhouse.

'But Bent Day should be for everyone! I *want* to go tomorrow.'

'No use talking like that, Janet. You heard your father last night. Girls cutting bent for thatch! Whatever next?'

She gives the pot one last polish with the rag. 'There. All ready for the new hearth chain.' Pride buzzes in her words.

I snort. Loudly. 'It'll only blacken again over the fire. And the other thing is, I'm stronger than George and William put together, Granna. It's a stupid rule!'

'Maybe,' she sings in her infuriating *no-point-arguing* voice.

I drop the subject before I'm tempted to launch myself at her neck and wring it; she *is* an old lady after all. The surf pounds the rocks down at the cove and the limited light from the tiny window takes on a golden tint. Late afternoon. I carry on pounding the grain to meal and imagine I'm grinding up stupid old rules until they blow away in the wind.

'When will they be back from Rispond, Granna?'

She shrugs, humming one of her tunes from Strathnaver again, and I know better than to ask any more. For the third time, I pick up the cat and ease it through the doorway back into the byre. *Silly beast. Always tries to get to the hearth.* Of course it loves the warmth of the fire—and who would blame it?

The sun hangs low over the horizon out west when, finally, I see them; Mother sitting on the mare and Father and Angus walking beside. The saddlebags are bulging. Am I imagining it, or is Angus taller than when I saw him this morning? *Nonsense, Janet! Surely he's stopped growing by now.* No-one looks much at their brother, mind, so I'll forgive myself for wondering. I throw the door wide.

'Keep the heat in!' croaks Granna, already dressed for the ceilidh and wrapped in the green wool blanket.

'They're back! At last.' I have been waiting for this moment.

4

'Janet; your father will be tired. Don't you go wearing him out now, will you lass?'

'What do you mean?' I fake outrage.

'You know fine! About the thatch-cutting tomorrow.'

'Oh, Granna; you know I'm not like that. Course I wouldn't!'

I try to look offended, but I suspect she knows very well that it *was* the very first thing I was going to mention.

'He'll be worn out from the road, lass. They all will.' She looks like she's going to say something else, but the mare's hoof beats already ring out across the cobbles by the Top House. They'll be down here in a few moments.

Rounding the bend above the beach, Father walks ahead of the other two.

'Janet.' It's a statement, a greeting, and his own gruff way of saying he notices me. When he squeezes the reins into my hands, it also becomes an order. I tie the mare to the post and hold my hand out. Mother slides down, clutching a folded bundle of cloth in one arm and a heavy rattling parcel in the other.

Granna is standing outside the house now, keeping the heat in quite forgotten. The sea breeze tugs at her knot of grey hair. 'So you got it.'

Mother looks weary. 'Yes, we got it, although it was three

tokens this time. That Master has no shame. If only he'd pay our men ordinary money. At least then we could trade at other places.'

Her voice drips with bitterness as she thrusts the clinking package into my grandmother's arms, but Granna hesitates to open it.

What are they still doing out here?

I don't want to look like I'm eavesdropping, so I loosen the saddle bags, ease them to the ground and reach for a handful of straw to start rubbing the mare down. *Say something, Janet.*

'What's in these, Mother? They're heavy.'

'This and that, mostly from Anderson's shop at Rispond. A couple of swapped things from Aunt Meg.' Mother stares at Granna who hasn't moved. 'What is it with you?'

'Did you bring… the other thing?'

Mother's forehead wrinkles like a triangle before she laughs. 'Oh, that! Yes, yes. I nearly forgot, but Angus reminded me. There… '

She fumbles through the folds of her skirt and produces a single sprig of fir. Its green needles' scent mingles with the salt in the air.

I open my mouth to speak, but think better of it when I see how everything about Granna turns fluid again. She hums as she hobbles into the house, package rattling under her arm and waving the fir sprig above her head like a flag of triumph.

'Ahem…' I begin, but Mother knows what I'm going to ask.

'Fir for luck, all the way from the woods at Strathmore. It's supposed to be wound into each new hearth chain. Don't make fun of her, Janet; it wouldn't be kind. Not after all she's been through. Your father says not to indulge it, but it means such a lot to her.'

By the time I've set the mare loose in the village grazing, dark clouds from the east chase the last afternoon rays. Our single candle on the table flickers as Granna stretches high on the chair to hang the new chain on the roof hook above the fire. A few blades of roof thatch sprinkle down on us.

'I wish you'd let me…' Father mumbles, but Granna is humming again, stopping only long enough to say 'Leave the hearth to the women, Johnnie!' Once the chain is secure, she fiddles around with it until the fir sprig is barely noticeable, right beneath the rafters where the smoke gathers. 'Shame we couldn't have afforded a thicker chain to hang the pot, like the Mackays up in the Top House.'

'Give it a rest, Mother.' Father barely looks up from his

ledger, carefully counting the tokens we have left and storing them again in the jar on the dresser. Granna clambers down to attach the scrubbed pot, but I get there before her and Father gives me an approving wink.

The soup soon simmers above the glimmering peat and I give the griddle a wipe before heating it for the first beremeal scone. Father stretches on the chair and inhales the wafting scent like fresh air. I take a deep breath. Granna and Mother shoot me a desperate warning look, but my chance is *now*, with Angus out of the way with the cattle.

'Father… about Bent Day tomorrow… '

CHAPTER THREE

The Ceilidh

I'M STILL IN A SULK WHEN THE FIRST OF US GATHER by the big fire beside the village soon after. Wee Donald from next door nestles up to me as Father and Mr Mackay from the Top House tune up the fiddles. It's a nice night; perfect for the ceilidh of stories and music that we have before every harvest, peat cutting—and Bent Day. My blood boils when I think of it. I'm just as capable of cutting some marram grass for thatch as any of the village boys.

Beside us, the burn splashes from the top of the hill past Ceannabeinne and down to the beach below. The tide's right out and the fish for grilling are lying in a basket by the fire already. I pull the blanket a little tighter round my shoulders when Wee Donald speaks at last.

'Wh-what is it, Janet?'

'You wouldn't understand.'

It gives me a stab of pain in my soul, the way he accepts

that answer. I wonder how often he hears it, or something like it. But no-one has a heart as sweet as Wee Donald, make no mistake, and that's got to count for something. Even if I'm in no mood to appreciate it right now.

Old Hugh Munro is making his way towards us and I stoke the fire to look busy.

'Are you going to give us a song then, Janet? To start the thing?'

I'm going to shake my head. He is the one who makes the rules in the village! He could unmake them, I'm sure—and let a keen, strong girl come to cut thatch.

Any second now I'm going to say no.

He's staring at me; I can feel it. Not unkindly, I suppose.

I take a deep breath, ready to say I'll sing—if he lets me go with them tomorrow.

And only then. But Hugh misunderstands my silence.

'Well done, Janet; we'll look forward to that. Good.'

Wee Donald nudges me to reply and I gather all my courage and look up, but the village elder has already turned and is talking to Granna.

I sigh. The waves roll in, claiming new territory with each advance, a few grains of sand at a time. More and more of us gather until almost fifty are here. From looking around, only Margaret Munro is missing, but she took a bad chill last week and probably wants to stay in bed.

Wish I had that choice. Or any choice, come to think of it, apart from churning butter and spinning and grinding flour. Taking the cattle to the hills is about the most adventurous it gets.

But oh, to go with the men to cut thatch at Balnakeil! It's just a few miles, I grant it; after all, we go to church there. Still, a day in the dunes, using the sickle like the boys. It's what I want.

A shred. A little shred of freedom.

I frown again until I feel Wee Donald rubbing my back. He notices things.

Mother, Father, Granna—even Angus—they're all the same, but Wee Donald listens. Now that his sister Catherine has gone to be a maid in Master Anderson's house, he is the only one left who doesn't irritate me—and I despise myself for it.

Thinking of Catherine makes me even more resentful. I miss her.

I know what I *should* do: try to be like Granna, hardworking and long-suffering, because Mother complains nearly as much as I do. Still, no-one ever tells *her* to wheesht. There—something else to complain about! Oh, I'm a hopeless case!

11

Wee Donald stirs and gets up, walking past the fire in such a lopsided way that I worry for a second, but no need. A murmur passes through the crowd and Father and Mr Mackay from the Top House play a short air on the fiddles to settle everyone before Hugh rises.

'We're all here tonight to ask the blessing of the good Lord on our venture tomorrow.'

I snort quietly and Granna gives me a kick from behind. 'What?' I hiss, rubbing my calf. *How does she do that? She was over by the MacIntoshes only a minute ago. It's impossible to put a toe out of line without Granna noticing!*

'So let us pray, both for that and... ' he hesitates, '...the issue which will be on our minds at this time.'

All around me, people bend their heads, although the gulls don't know anything about proper reverence, shrieking on regardless. My mind swirls like the sea. *Other thing? What other thing? Is anyone ill? Is it the cattle? Or something wrong with the grain? But no, I don't think it's that; I was down there earlier this week and all looks just as it's always done.*

Granna pokes my back from behind. *How does she always, always know?* With a sigh I close my eyes, wait for Hugh Munro to finish and pronounce my *Amen* as loudly and clearly as I can, glancing over my shoulder. Granna looks away but gives an approving nod all the same. At least I hope it's approving.

Hugh looks over at me. 'And now our most promising young singer is going to give us a wee tune.'

Father winks and plays his two middle strings once to give me a starting note. I try not to think about it. If I think about it, my voice scurries away and hides under the stones like a mouse. Instead, I lift my eyes to the darkening sky and the melody lifts me away with it like a soaring eagle. It's a short one, only three verses, all about the land and the sea. I finish and Granna's hand is on my shoulder again, clawing in hard, but not in a mean way. I turn my head and tears are streaming down her face. I'm not surprised. Music does that to her, unless it's a jig.

Come to think of it, even jigs make her cry sometimes.

It all reminds her. I wish there was something I could do, but she's got all her wits about her still. And all her memories. Which, in *her* case, is *not* a good thing.

I squeeze her hand back and feel a little of my annoyance drain away.

Next comes a reel and even though the patch of land here isn't entirely flat, most of us are on our feet. Wee Donald gets to me first and I do the *Strip the Willow* with him, even though I can see Hector Mackay scowl at us across the flames. Why on earth doesn't he ask Peggy if he's so desperate to dance?

Two dances and a story of the seal people later, I can't hold a grudge any longer; the music and the words simply carry it away. As the tide splashes closer, Hector and Angus have to raise their voices to sing their own ballad; the wind picks up and the bere grain rustles in the fields beyond the village. Granna recites her favourite poem, the Schoolmaster gives some news of the kingdom, and Hugh Munro finishes with a prayer before dismissing us:

'Bright and early for Bent Day, mind! I'll send the women to knock on doors. You young lads, Angus and Hector, you'll get the horses and the carts ready, will ye? The folks from the island are crossing at sunrise, so we'd best be ready when they get here. We'll need the whole day. Let's pray for the weather to stay fair, and thank ye all.'

The dispersal of the crowd is almost instant, but Granna and I stay for a few more minutes to watch. The flames fight on for a wee while, but in the end, they die down.

'I love a wood fire, Granna. The peat on our hearth burns so low; more like a glow. Driftwood burns so brightly. Isn't it braw?'

I help her trace her steps back to the house, but Granna says nothing and once I realise, I feel like an idiot. Of course she doesn't love it—she told me all about those days. I can't help it; my mind imagines what she must be remembering at this moment:

Sparks screaming into the night sky.

The inferno.

I sink onto my straw mattress without another word, but Angus's and Father's snores are well into their nightly duet before I can banish these images from my head.

Chapter Four

Bent Day

ANGUS IS ALREADY UP BY THE TIME A FRAGILE RAY OF LIGHT battles its way through my lids. I gasp and stretch, resulting in a frightening sound which makes even Granna sit up. I can't help smiling, her hair at all angles like that and eyes wide—until I remember what day it is today. Then *not* smiling becomes very, very easy. I kick back against her box bed, rise from my straw mattress by the hearth, clang the empty pot hard against the low table as I pass, rattling the chain for good measure and wrap the blanket around me. Without glancing back once, I sweep out of the house, gasping at the chill in the air, and stomp towards the spring. There's already a queue.

Even though it's barely light, Mrs Mackay from the Top House has her hair arranged like something you could display in Master Anderson's mansion. *Éist! That must have taken her hours! I wonder whether she even went to bed at all after the ceilidh.*

Without thinking, my hands shoot up to my head and flatten my own hair, hanging all the way down my back in its stubborn auburn defiance. 'A lion would be proud of that,' the Schoolmaster once said, pointing at my hair on what *I* thought was quite a tidy day. I've never quite forgiven him for that. Even if he did follow it by saying I had the voice of an angel. Who does he think he is! As if *he* saw angels and lions every other day.

I feel a tapping on my shoulder. It's just Wee Donald behind me with a bucket for his byre.

'Morning,' I grunt, even though I know fine that none of this is *his* fault. Then, suddenly, an awful possibility strikes me and I blanch. 'Donald, are you going with the men today? Thatch-cutting? Are you?'

He does that thing he often does. Oh, very well, that thing he *always* does, where he looks like he doesn't understand a word you're saying. His eyes scrunch up and I can almost see the wheels turning while his brain tries to match my words to meanings. I repeat my question more slowly. 'Are you going to Balnakeil with the men today? To cut bent for thatch?'

'Cut thatch,' he answers. He waits, takes a deep breath and smiles. The sea of rage in my stomach simmers up again. 'S-staying here with you,' he finally announces, simultaneously giving me a gentle nudge towards the spring.

Oh yes—my turn to fill the pot. The Seamstress behind me gives a scowl. What's *her* hurry, I wonder?

Just as well Wee Donald is staying in the village. If he was allowed to go, it would only add insult to injury, given that I'm four years older and I'm at least twice as strong. The peaty water splashes into the pot and as I watch, I hate myself for begrudging Wee Donald anything at all, especially now that he has been thrown out of school. I shiver at the memory of the Schoolmaster's words: 'There is simply no point in trying to teach someone like that,' he said, but he couldn't hide his glee, vile man that he is. Wee Donald would be able to teach that Schoolmaster a thing or two about kindness.

I wait for my friend and we stagger back together. When I see the way he stumbles along with that pail, I wonder if there'll be any water left for their cattle at the other end.

A little over an hour later, the sun has set off on its journey towards the big blue above, and we gather to bid farewell to the Bent Day party. Master Anderson of Rispond has given all the seagoing men the day off to help, though it'll mean no pay. Father looked at the ledger again this morning, something brooding in his face. I saw it.

I'm sure he knows that I saw, because he reached over in a hurry, opening the Bible and leaving it open on the table for me to read to Granna and Mother later.

Now he leads the long line of men. The mare and the old stallion pull a cart each; one borrowed from the Rispond Estate. I doubt that was free either. Granna and Mother both wave, and I take care to arrange my stance in such a way that, even from a distance, it'll look angry and resentful: hand on hip, face slightly turned away. It's all wasted, however. Angus just laughs and points, elbowing Hector to join in.

Father doesn't look back once.

I storm back inside the house, climb through into the byre and start mucking out. It feels good driving the cattle to pasture a little way up the hill afterwards, jabbing the beasts into submission with the cattle prod usually wielded by my brother. It weighs heavy in my hand and knocks me off balance once as I clamber upwards across rock.

'Morning, Janet,' calls Mary Mackie, one of Mother's friends. Her two boys are off with the men, of course.

'Morning, Mary. You're early.' I tug at my plait, self-conscious all of a sudden, but the woman's face is bright. She isn't the disapproving kind, anyway. I let go of my hair.

'It's a good day for the thatch-cutting, eh Janet? Gives us a bit of peace from the men, doesn't it?' She smiles easily, and if she means her boys, I suppose she's right. *How long since her husband was drowned? Before my time, that's all I know.*

'Yes, I suppose it does.' I smile back. 'There is plenty of pasture here. I don't usually go up this way much, only Angus. But that might change if Anderson will have him for the boatbuilding. There's talk of that.'

My Lord; that must have been the longest speech I've made to an adult other than Granna in my life. But Mary's a kind soul, and she never says a bad word about Wee Donald which makes her worth speaking to in my book.

'That would help. That would certainly help, would it not, Janet?' A shadow crosses her face before she breathes deeply. 'So, are you going to carry on at the schoolhouse?'

'Not that much longer.' *I hope,* I add on in the secret depth of my heart, but I might as well have said it aloud.

'We never had such blessings, Janet. Don't resent them.'

Before I can think of a clever answer to that, she continues. 'And I think you should head back down. I'll take care of all the cattle. I've only the three left now the bull's gone, so yours will make it worth my while staying.'

I hesitate.

20

'Honestly, it's no trouble. You can take over after dinner if you want, but I'll be fine, and your grandmother will be wanting you.'

Oh, yes. I don't doubt Granna could think of a job or two to keep me occupied.

'All right then. If you're sure you don't mind, Mary.'

'I'm certain. And you don't need to hurry. I won't say anything.' She winks.

I stammer my thanks and head down the hill the long way, bending down to check for nests in the heather and letting the breeze caress my cheeks. The waves in the distance roll in like a heartbeat, steady and strong. I count the skylarks, scanning the landscape for the eagle from the Ben at the same time.

Hang on. What's that?

A rider; still some way off. Not in a hurry, I think, but heading towards us on the Tongue Road.

I wait for my head to assemble the pieces. Both the horses from Ceannabeinne are at the thatch cutting at Balnakeil with our men, miles away along the coast in the opposite direction. That man is wearing a fancy hat; I can tell that even from here.

So. This is *not* one of *our* men on one of *our* horses.

Of course, he might just be passing through, going to

Smoo or Sangomore or Durine. But usually, visitors go as far as Anderson's estate at Rispond and no further, which means we don't even see them.

I try to recall the last time I saw a strange lone rider on that road. What could he possibly want?

Unless…

Granna's tales of riders gallop, unbidden, into my mind. *Oh Lord!*

Hugh's words echo in my ears—*'the issue which will be on our minds at this time'*—and I break into a trot. Before long I'm hurtling down the hill through the heather and stumble onto the road beside the schoolhouse, at the very moment the rider rounds the bend. I don't even feel my legs bleeding, scratched by bracken.

It's just as I feared; he's holding a letter. Is that a Sheriff's uniform? It might all be innocent, of course, but I simply can't take that risk—not knowing what I do about Granna.

He's probably seen me, but I don't care.

Then the most awful truth hits me.

All the men are away. Even the Schoolmaster.

There is no-one here to defend us.

Panic lends me wings as I fly down the path and I fear I'm going to beat down the wooden door of the Top House, so desperate are my knocks.

Chapter Five

The Writ

I'M ABOUT TO START SCREAMING WHEN THE DOOR OPENS at last and Peggy appears, holding a half-finished pleated pigtail. I lose no time at all.

'Where's your mother?'

'Gone to see the Seamstress,' she sneers, even though she's only eleven. 'Why?'

We hear him before we see him: the sound of hooves is suddenly sharper as the rider turns down from the road and the cobbles give away how close he is now. Only the Top House has cobbles of course. They slow the rider down, which is a blessing, but I'm unable to either move or speak. Peggy drops her hair and the plait falls out.

'Ho there,' a man's voice rings out. It's too near for comfort.

When he comes into view, he seems unbearably tall: on

23

his horse, in his uniform, with his hat.

We don't answer, but he simply speaks on. 'I'm Sheriff Officer Campbell, here on important business. Take me to Hugh Munro, if you'd be so kind.'

Peggy doesn't seem too worried, simply sighs, steps over the threshold and approaches the man. I follow her, praying and begging the good Lord for it to be something else. Mind, I can't think of anything good it could be at all. The horse looks even higher once I'm standing right in front of him, and the man hasn't got a stain on his jacket. Only the worst kind of men have no stains on their coats, Granna says. His eyes, however, are not unkind. 'Where be Hugh Munro's house, lass?'

'Mr Munro lives down in the cottages, but he is not here, Sir,' curtsies Peggy, trying to be cute and polite. I step back, eyeing the piece of paper in his hand.

'Is that so,' he says. It's not a question, and that worries me more than anything else.

'I've a writ to deliver. Since he's the elder, I'll best give it to his good lady. Could you show me the house?' He does something with the corners of his mouth. I'm sure it's meant to be a smile, but his eyes are serious. Even sad.

A writ? Just like Granna had a writ once.

He said "writ".

24

I've got to run. Find Granna. Find Mother. Oh Lord…

'I'll show you the way if you like, Sir,' volunteers Peggy, doing the thing she does, being the princess of sweetness to adults she thinks are important.

'Don't touch it!' I hiss under my breath. 'Whatever you do, don't touch that paper, that much I know!' I push past her and past the man on the horse, who looks bewildered and anguished now. On the way, I dig my sharpest fingernail into the horse's flank and it leaps forward, rears and canters off.

'Bolt the door, Peggy, if you know what's good for you. For all of us!'

The fifty yards to our house have never felt further. I yell, all the way. Not words exactly; only sounds of fear and helplessness.

Doors open. Hens scatter. Still I scream. Out of breath, I come to a standstill before Granna while Mother hurries over from the field. I want to explain, I really do, but I don't think I need to. Granna's face is frozen in terror. Mother's run has slowed to a walk and she puts her arm round us both.

'What a cowardly, cowardly thing to do,' she mumbles.

Back in control of his mount, the rider approaches our gathering group of women and children.

The horse stands still now.

'Good day to you all. My name is Sheriff Officer Campbell. Some of you may know me. I've come to deliver this eviction writ to the village of Ceannabeinne.'

He coughs a little, but starts reading in an official, sing-songy voice that reminds me of the Reverend. 'The good folk of Ceannabeinne are required to leave the township within forty-eight hours hence. This is by law and order due to instruction by Master Anderson of Rispond, tacksman and holder of tenancy over all subtenants, present or not…' His voice cracks.

Leave Ceannabeinne? In less than 2 days? This is even worse than I imagined!

'This is the devil's work. How can you be part of it?' The Seamstress steps forward while Mrs Mackay stays back in the shadows of the cottage. Cuts of printed cotton still hang arranged over her shoulder, making her stand out against all the rest of us in our dull woollen clothes.

'Please, good lady, show me the Munro house and leave me be. I mean you no harm. Your township isn't the only one.'

Old Isabella Matheson from the beach cottage reaches us, out of breath, her ankles sprayed with mud. She must have shuffled right through the burn instead of going the long way. Despite that, her voice is steady when she addresses the stranger.

'Why don't you come down from that horse, Sir? You see, Mrs Munro isn't keeping well. You'll kill her with fright if she sees you on that steed.'

The man hesitates, but then exhales for a long time, and loosens his reins. Isabella nods, looking at her feet. In a sudden, slick movement, he swings his leg over the horse's rear.

I gasp, but Mother nudges me. Her voice is choked. 'There's nothing we can do, Janet. What will be, will be.'

The women take a step back, but Granna goes all the way back into the house, as if she can't bear it. Isabella smiles, sweet and welcoming, but we all know she's not like that at all. If she's frightened, she doesn't show it. She is buying us all time. To think.

Think, Janet!

The man's heavy black boot makes a thud on the compact mud as an idea forms in my mind.

I think of Granna's silhouette, framed for a second in the bright sun before disappearing into the darkness of the house. Stooped, miserable—defeated already.

I hurl myself at the Sheriff Officer who still has one foot in his stirrup, his free hand clenching the writ. My head hits him on the arm, just below the shoulder and he tumbles to the ground. I fall sideways, recoiling from the piece of paper. Isabella is the first to catch on and she kneels on his arm. Mother and the Seamstress and the Lord knows who else all pile in, weighing him down. Granna's face reappears at the door. My throat hurts more than I've ever known, but I manage to cry out over the din. 'Fire, Granna. Bring fire. And a knife.' Her eyes widen, but she rushes inside and all I can do is help hold the man down. Even with five of us and Wee Donald—*where did he come from?*—we struggle to keep the man on the ground, three knees pinning down the arm holding the writ. In the end, it's Isabella who presses Father's fish-gutting knife to his throat.

'Get up! Back to the road so that we can send you on your way. And take your writ away with you!' Fury is spilling out through every crack and wrinkle of her weathered face. 'And don't you think I'm joking either.'

Mary appears by the road. She must have heard the noise.

'Quick, run up the hill and shout for the men, Mary!' Isabella commands. 'The wind is going the right way. Wee Donald can look after the cattle later!'

No-one would have the courage to argue with Isabella, and Mary is no exception. When I see her hurrying up the hill by the sea, I can barely believe she is no more than two years younger than Mother. We have only pulled the cursing man halfway back up the path towards the road when her voice rings out, louder than I could have ever imagined. *Will it reach as far as Balnakeil?* I don't know. Mother's hair is half bun and half lion's mane, and when I see her now I think that maybe we do have some things in common after all.

The man's curses fade to pleas, but six of us claw into his arm, forcing him to hold the writ out ahead. Isabella and the Seamstress have taken charge by the time the feeble Mrs Munro finally emerges from her house. 'Stay a good distance away, Margaret,' Isabella shouts, and I wonder at her strength, given that she's almost sixty and walks with a limp. 'We can't let him serve the writ. I know his kind, same as Anna there, too. And trust me; you don't want to let him touch you with that paper of the devil. Those days are gone!' She addresses that last sentence to the man himself who is probably already trying to work out how to tell his master that he's been dragged out of Ceannabeinne by a bunch of old women and children. I look round. Mrs Mackay from the Top House, Peggy and Margaret Munro are following at a distance.

Fine. Let them stand back. We don't need their help!

'That should do it, Anna,' Isabella wheezes. 'Janet's right.

All you young folk, get some tinder—any driftwood or dry bracken you can find. And be quick, so I can put this monster out of his misery and send him back to Anderson with his sorry tale.'

Granna has carried the whole smouldering piece of peat from the hearth in a bucket. She empties it onto a hastily assembled bed of rocks. Peggy throws on a handful of dried twigs, Wee Donald adds some dry grass, and smoke rises to the heavens like our cry for help.

'Burn the writ,' the Seamstress commands the man. She is holding the knife now, all trace of her usual jollity gone from her voice.

'You know I can't. I've got to serve it.' His face is a map of pain, and I feel sorry for him for a moment. Until I remember what he's here to do. Anderson's devil work!

'Give me that.' Isabella grabs the knife, and instead of pointing it at his back as she did to force him up the hill, she presses it right into his throat. Even I can't watch as the skin yields. A small trickle of blood appears, taking the long route down his neck before soaking into the Sheriff Officer's white shirt.

'Leave off, Isabella. We don't want you guilty of murder...,' the Seamstress says as she pushes the knife down to point at his chest, '...unless absolutely necessary.'

A deathly pallor spreads across the man's face and he freezes.

'Is it really an eviction writ, Granna? Does it mean we have to leave?' I wheeze, still holding on to the man's arm.

But Granna ignores me and startles all of us, even Isabella, with the daggers in her voice. 'We have to *make* him burn it, whatever it takes. I stood by once. Not this time.'

We hesitate, but not long. In a desperate effort, we drag him once more—but this time towards the fire, now bright by the roadside, all shouting at once.

'Lower!'

'He's so heavy!'

'Force his arm!'

'Almost…'

The Sheriff Officer writhes, still clinging on to the writ. 'You'll regret this. Leave me be! He'll only send it again. I'm not saying it's right, but Mr Anderson can do as he pleases, and if he wants to empty the villages, he can. You know that yourselves!' His voice squirms with him, high and gasping, but it's no use. I grit my teeth as I pull his arm over the fire, clawing my nails into his skin so hard he yelps in pain.

'That should do it, Janet. Good girl.' Isabella almost grunts these words, clinging onto the man's shoulder and

31

still pointing the knife at his chest.

I can smell the singed hairs on his arm and feel the urge to be sick. *Nearly; so nearly...*

The sleeve of my dress starts to smoke, but I pull his hand over the highest flame and bite my lip not to scream.

In the end, the movement is miniscule, almost not there at all. I know he's let go by the exhaling all around me. As if by instinct, we all pull back and he leaps away from the fire like a man possessed; his eyes wild. The writ fights the greedy flames; contorts and dodges, but it is no use.

The fire devours it. There is nothing left but ash.

What have we done to the servant of the law? His hat lies crumpled, still halfway down the path. His breeches are torn, his shirt blood-stained at the neck. I stand well back, but now I'm not so sure how pleased I should be with our handiwork. And what would Father say? If he could see Mother now, standing beside me, her hand on my shoulder.

The gulls scream their outrage to the sky, but we are all out of voice.

Except Isabella.

'Mind, that writ was never served.'

She croaks it, and turns to go, but the man nods. He sinks down by the roadside while we stand around him with funeral faces. I wouldn't want to be in his shoes, and it's taken me till now to realise.

'I'll get your horse,' the Seamstress finally says, as if she hadn't held a knife to his heart only moments before. Mother gathers up the weapon, discarded on the ground, and pulls me and Granna along the path with her. 'Let's allow him some dignity. I know his face. He's from over Eriboll way somewhere.'

But I resist because I need to hear the truth. 'Granna, did you know about this before?'

Mother looks straight ahead.

'Mother? Granna? Please answer me. Did you know this was going to happen? Is that what Hugh Munro was talking about when he led the prayer?'

Granna keeps walking, but Mother sighs. 'We had a formal notice in the spring. It said that the land had to be cleared for sheep farming by Whitsun.'

She is about to continue, but I can't let her yet. My questions tumble around in my head like rocks in the river, heavy and hard. 'So he really wants us to leave? What, all of us, like what happened to Granna? I thought those days were over?'

'So did we. No-one expected Anderson to go through with it. We heard nothing more, for weeks and thought he might have changed his mind. After all, he's selling fish as far as Russia, and the men have worked hard for him. So we were hoping that it would all come to nothing. That he would let us stay...'

And then her tears come, as the enormity of what we have just done sinks in. 'Oh, Janet, think! If you hadn't seen him and given us warning, we'd be served with a writ now and we'd have to be gone in two days. And we've nowhere to go, nowhere at all. And all the men away. Anderson knew fine well, that's why he sent the officer today.'

I shift, slightly uncomfortable with suddenly being my mother's best friend. I reach for her hand. 'But we saw him off, didn't we, Mother? We taught him a lesson he won't forget.'

If this was supposed to cheer her up, it seems to achieve quite the opposite.

'But, don't you realise,' she sobs. 'This is the beginning of the end.'

Shouts by the roadside alert us to the fact that some of the men are returning, but the dishevelled rider has already disappeared over the schoolhouse hill, no doubt trotting back to Rispond to tell Master Anderson. Mother hurriedly fixes her hair back into a bun and smooths her singed apron.

'There'll be a meeting, no doubt. Janet, I'm going to see to Granna.' She squeezes my shoulder and vanishes into the house. I squint back along the coast towards Smoo, and right enough, there are some runners, hastening towards us.

Could Mary's voice really have carried that far?

It must have. Angus and Hector Mackay are among the first, as well as young Eric Mackie, Mary's boy, and I'm not sure about the fourth. *Maybe someone from the island?* On impulse, I turn and scramble up the schoolhouse hill, leaning against the Big Boulder to catch my breath. I just catch sight of the rider in the distance, turning off the Tongue Road towards Rispond. His posture is hunched.

My thirteenth birthday is only two months away. But however much I thought I wanted adventure, now that it may be thrust upon me, I am certain of one thing:

I do not want it anymore.

Strathnaver 1814: The Writ

'The man is a devil, make no mistake.'

John never spoke like that, never. Anna turned her face away and pulled Wee Johnnie back from the hearth for the hundredth time that morning.

'No, Johnnie, stop it! You don't play with the fire! It's

dangerous. Out you go.'

The boy toddled into the sunshine.

'So, you're sure it's a writ, John? Did you see it for yourself?'

'Yes. You won't be able to read it, even if you could read, Anna—it's all in English. Whitsun it is. Murdo doesn't think he's serious, but I would put nothing past Patrick Sellar. As I say, the man is a devil. But this is our land. There may be a bit of paper in his legal office to say that he can do as he pleases, but we're staying. This is our home.'

John scratched his beard and put the paper under the pot on the sideboard, pulling his weathered hand away as if the paper itself was possessed.

The sun took that very moment to wriggle its way through the narrow window into their longhouse. It was hard to think that what had been threatened really could happen: men on horses, brandishing weapons and banishing their little family from their home. Pulling down the stones that John had hauled, one on top of the other. Burning the thatch that he had cut.

'He'll see sense, John. You always make everything seem so bleak.'

'The man is a devil.'

'Hush, John. The child.'

Both of them looked at the boy in the doorway, set to farm this land after his father, to live in this house or build one like it, find a wife, settle in the village and work as his father had before him.

'Oh, John…' Anna bit her lower lip and hummed a tune to keep away the tears. 'What will become of us?'

CHAPTER SIX

The Meeting

ONE BY ONE, THEY TRICKLE IN. ANGUS FIRST; ALWAYS THE RUNNER. Hector and Mary's boys follow together and then the men. Father leads one of the carts, only a quarter full of bent for the thatch.

I suppose there's no point now, is there? Who thatches a house only to watch it set alight?

To my surprise, Angus does not turn down the path towards the house but heads up the hill. This hill.

Towards me.

'Janet.'

He's so like Father; he can't even give a proper greeting. My name can be it all: a complaint, a rebuke, a word of affection, a thank you. But today it's something else. It holds all the anguish and tension and compassion of a young man who feels he should have *been there*. For Mother, for Granna, and yes, also for me.

He waits, never one for many words. Never one for excitement or fits of rage. Sometimes I wonder that we're related at all. He's caught the sun, his face redder and frecklier than usual. Still he waits.

'The Sheriff Officer came. To serve a writ.'

He nods. Of course, they would have guessed after Mary's call.

'We made him burn it, Angus.'

Now, that's got his attention all right. He looks up sharp.

'He burnt it?'

'He didn't get much choice in the matter.' Both of us can't quite suppress a grin, looking down at the heather beneath our feet. 'He went back to Rispond. The writ wasn't served, but this isn't the end of it, is it?'

I don't have to say any more. The glen at Strathnaver was cleared with such terrible cruelty. Granna can hardly bear to talk about it.

The villages along the coast at Eriboll were next. Not as long ago; not so brutal—but evicted nonetheless. All this continued to the west. With every village cleared, some of the people settled in Ceannabeinne, invited by Anderson and his father before him. After all, they needed workers for the fisheries at Rispond and the boatbuilding.

And surely, Anderson's business is thriving.

Isn't it?

'None of us believed it would happen here.' Angus's words seem distant, so far have I drifted in my thoughts.

I shake my head. 'So what now?' I play with the burnt hem of my sleeve and wonder what the Sheriff Officer's sleeves look like. I wonder if his burns sting like mine.

'There'll be a meeting, I wager.' Angus pulls himself up and leans against the Big Boulder. Below us in the village, people run in and out of each other's houses like ants. The horses are set loose to graze, the bent for the thatch is taken into the outbuilding by the burn. And still men stand, crowding in small groups, while women relay the tale, again and again. I can see a couple of lads from the island getting ready to row across, no doubt letting the folks there know—only four families, but still. Them too.

'I'm going down. So should you, Janet. Granna will be in a bad way.'

I sigh.

'Don't be selfish. You'll be wanted.' He speaks with the authority of an adult, so much so that I sometimes forget he's only three years older than me. I rise and run after him.

Normally meetings take time to call. A messenger is sent, a time proposed and agreed, work is finished and set aside. Clothing is tidied, hair brushed. In orderly fashion, we make our way to the school up by the road.

Not this time. We meet by the whitewashed building within minutes of the last man's arrival. Hector Mackay has been sent to fetch the minister from Balnakeil, but otherwise, everyone is here, I think. The Schoolmaster beckons us in. 'Old people first; don't you young lot take their seats. Make room for the women, for goodness' sake. Stay back Janet! Must you always be the one?'

'I'm helping Granna find a seat!' I snap. I want to call him an ignorant hog, but I suspect that wouldn't go down well, least of all now. Father stands against the back wall, one arm around Mother, scratching his beard with the other, while Angus is crouching somewhere on the floor at the front. I can't see many of the young folk from here, but I'd better stay with Granna. A wooden box stands at the front, and Hugh Munro is on it before we've had a chance to settle.

'So, he's served a writ, has he? Wants us off the land, does he?' All of us are taken aback by the fire in his voice, and him normally such a mild-mannered sort. A true gentleman, whatever they may call Anderson of Rispond.

'Well, you can only push folk so far. And this, I say, is far enough! All of us have gone through hardships, some more than others. And in the end, it comes down to this.

Ye don't give us shelter, only to RIP IT OFF FROM OVER OUR HEADS!'

I wince at his fury, despite the fact it's the truth, of course.

'Hugh, he's got every right. That's the problem,' sneers the Schoolmaster. Only he would interrupt Hugh Munro like that, his nasal voice in sharp contrast with Hugh's low rumble.

'There's right by the devil's law, and then there's right by the Lord. I think we can all tell the difference.' Hugh's breath comes in short rasps. 'Now, we need to hear the story, as it happened. Nothing added in, nothing left out. From the moment the Sheriff Officer was first spotted. Who can do that for us?'

And, as the seconds tick by, all eyes come to rest on me.

The Schoolmaster rolls his eyes.

'Go on, Janet.' Hugh Munro is back to his usual self, speaking his low, melodious encouragement right into my heart. My stomach churns like butter, but Granna and Mother both nod, and I have no choice but to begin.

I wish they didn't, but the tears come, especially when I describe how Granna fetched the fire in the pail. I hold back my sleeve to show the reddened blisters which no doubt have distant twins on Sheriff Officer Campbell's arms. Old Margaret Munro averts her eyes. I finish by telling of the rider turning down the road to Rispond.

In the silence that follows, I wonder. I am a girl, only twelve years of age, but not once was I interrupted. That doesn't stop the Schoolmaster from offering an opinion now.

'Well, it can only be lamented how foolishly the womenfolk acted in the absence of the men.'

Isabella shakes her head. 'Who are you calling foolish, young Schoolmaster?' she rasps.

I've never thought of the Schoolmaster as a young man, but I suppose he is, compared to Isabella, who now squares up to him like for a fight of fisticuffs, her voice shaking. 'Are we just to take the writ and start packing? Is that what you want? You, the most comfortably off in the school cottage here, with wages and all?'

He's not the most comfortably off, and I bet that Mrs Mackay from the Top House wants to tell everyone so, but she doesn't get the chance.

'*Feasgar math.* How are you all?' The Reverend Findlater has arrived, still out of breath, but exuding the calm authority he always does. Instantly, I feel like I'm in church. I'm sure everyone else is the same.

Hugh shakes his hand. 'Thank you for coming, Minister. We have terrible news. A writ was sent today when all the menfolk were at Balnakeil cutting bent for thatch. But it wasn't served. The women forced him to burn it. And that's the long and short of it.'

A shadow of pain crosses the minister's face. 'He will be angry.' The Reverend shakes his head. 'The Master Anderson. He'll be very angry.'

'We worked that out for ourselves!' the Seamstress says under her breath, but no-one laughs.

The Minister's face is deadly serious. 'Did you say force was used against a servant of the law?'

A memory of a picture in a school book flits through my mind: Dornoch jail.

'Servant of the devil, more like.' *Éist, is the Seamstress not even awed by such a man of God?*

'They all joined in.' Hugh Munro says.

'Not all,' the Mackays from the Top House protest.

'Almost all,' says Hugh, correcting himself. 'But only two held the knife to the man. Isabella and Mrs Morrison, the Seamstress.' Hugh shakes his head. 'I wish tae the Lord this had never happened. For these two women may now be in danger on account of the whole village.'

I look at Granna. Her face is grave.

Hugh continues. 'So we need to decide two things. What's to be done about the women in question? And what's to be done about Anderson and the writ?'

He sways a little and the Minister sits him down.

'I think…' begins the Schoolmaster, but the Reverend rises and lifts his hands in prayer.

All of us stand, even Granna and unwell Margaret Munro, and we close our eyes while the minister pleads for God's mercy in our hour of need, and for wisdom, and probably lots of other things, only I'm not hearing them because my mind wanders, however hard I try. I make up for it with the most heartfelt *Amen* in the room.

It's a darkening sky by the time the islanders row back across to Eilean Hoan and we see to the cattle in the byre. I give the cat a shallow bowl of milk as soon as Mother is gone and it rewards me by curling up into my lap. A little while later, I go into the garden to gather the ripe berries before they spoil, and I wonder how he's getting on—the Minister, down at Rispond, pleading our cause to the Master Anderson. The candlelight in the Seamstress's cottage is bright. It was decided that she and Isabella will leave for the hill cave at first light, in case the Sheriff Officers come for them. They may have to stay some time.

And, stumbling back under a charcoal sky, I think about what my part will be.

Tomorrow.

When I turn spy.

CHAPTER SEVEN

The Master's House

'AND T-TAKE THIS TO THE M-MASTER'S HOUSE, TOO,' SAYS Wee Donald holding up a knitted woollen blanket.

I groan. 'Do I have to? Catherine will be having a day off soon. And I have more important things to do.'

'Our m-mother says she must have it.' Wee Donald looks up at me with his lopsided smile.

I can't resist when he looks up at me like that, and he knows it.

'Donald, I'm supposed to be a spy, not a pack-horse. Just don't you tell another soul that I agreed to carry things for Catherine, otherwise every man and woman and child will think of something they want me to fetch from Anderson's shop. Promise?'

'P-promise.'

Wee Donald makes a fist and thumps his chest like I imagine a pagan warrior might. He must think that it makes him look solemn, like he really means it. I haven't the heart to tell him otherwise.

But the next thing he says catches me by surprise.

'Janet, what's h-happening to us all?'

It's a simple question. And I sigh. Of course he doesn't understand. For him, *not* understanding is perfectly ordinary. How can I tell him that *we* all don't understand either?

I begin. 'Master Anderson of Rispond. Catherine's master…'

'Yes?' His forehead wrinkles with concentration.

'He is the one who controls the land. He's got the lease. He has sort of… borrowed it from the owner.'

'The D-Duke?'

'Yes. But it's Anderson who makes all the decisions.'

Wee Donald pauses. Finally, he nods. His wide eyes are on me.

'And now, Anderson has decided to put us all out of our homes. He wants all the land back so he can put sheep on it.'

Wee Donald laughs and I give him a frustrated shove. 'It's not funny. Really! When Granna and Isabella were young, the same happened. Only that time there was another, really evil master: a Mr Patrick Sellar. People died, Donald! They burnt the houses, sometimes over the people's heads.'

Now this stops Wee Donald's giggles at once. There is a pause while he takes it all in.

'Why sh-sheep?'

'They bring in more money than fishing. And we are in the way.'

He opens his mouth to speak but closes it again, his face a mask of disappointment.

'I still d-don't understand.'

I ruffle his hair. 'Me neither. Now, get busy. The boys will need help with the cattle on the hillside before long. Is it your turn to bring the milk down?'

'Yes,' he says, matter-of-fact, before he works out what I've just said. 'Oh, L-Lord, it is, isn't it?' He jumps up from the low chair, skirts round our hearth in the middle of the room and runs to the small window, squinting to see the sun. 'I'm late and n-no mistake!' He shoots out of the doorway, nearly knocking Granna over as she tries to come in from the garden.

Strathnaver 1814: Like a Ghost

High on his horse. High on the hill. High and mighty, above her and all she loved.

Anna narrowed her eyes, but it was the Factor, Patrick

Sellar, without doubt, looking down from the hilltop. Tomorrow was to be the day.

Maybe, if he saw the hard work of the tenants, he'd change his mind. Or was he already imagining the hills without the people, without the houses, even without the runrigs where they grew their bere? Rolling hills and green valleys, dotted with sheep? What was the Duchess of Sutherland thinking, entrusting the running of her whole estate to such a man?

Anna felt a sudden pang of guilt. What about forgiving our debtors as it said in the Bible? She uttered a mumbled prayer for the man silhouetted against the evening sky, and then another, much more heartfelt, for her John, Wee Johnnie and the whole village.

Maggie Mackay next door was sick again, shaken by the fever. People in the village said she was ninety years of age, but that simply couldn't be, could it?

Earlier today, a group of elders from the Strathnaver villages had gone to plead with Sellar, but he had refused to even see them. 'A sure sign that his conscience is troubling him,' she had said to John, but he had shaken his head.

A gentle caress to her calves startled her and she bent down to stroke the cat.

And like a ghost, the man on top of the hill was gone.

*

'Look, Janet. The cabbages are coming on well.' There is a false cheerfulness about Granna, but I'll take that over misery.

'Good,' I answer.

'We'll be able to swap some—there are too many for the five of us to eat. Maybe we can get some wool from the Top House. How many sheep have they got again?'

'Only two now; the black lamb died. Do the Top House Mackays eat cabbage?'

'There's no-one doesn't eat cabbage, Janet. Not when they're this good!' She turns to tend the fire.

'I'd better be on my way to the Master's house, Granna.'

'God be with you.' As if on second thought, she reaches up high and twists the fir twig in the chain, already dried and blackened. She rubs a needle or two in her hands so I can smell it and then brushes the scent over my head, hair and shoulders.

'There, Janet darling. Fir for luck.'

I try to smile; my lips tight.

I nearly stumble over the cat on my way out and Donald's bundle makes me unsteady as I walk up the path, past the Top House where, no doubt, Mrs Mackay is arranging her locks in front of the looking glass. Once I reach the road, I sling the bundle over my shoulder and climb towards the school. No-one's there today. The Schoolmaster has gone out to discuss "matters in hand" with people in the villages to the west—as if Sangomore or Durine or anyone else could make a difference. It's Anderson we have to talk to, and if he won't even listen to the Reverend, then what hope have we got?

Still, at least I'm doing something. And doing something feels good. Forget thatch-cutting: now they trust me with one of the most important jobs there is—and I can do it much better than Angus or Hector or any of the boys.

I round school hill and head towards Rispond. Hundreds of feet below me, the breakers fight their daily battle with the sands.

'Can I help you at all?'

I take a step back. This is not the cook who normally answers the kitchen door and I'm flummoxed. I try to look harmless but useful. Not easy.

'My name is Janet Sutherland. I've come to see Catherine McRae. She's one of the kitchen maids. Is she free for a moment?'

The woman snorts, and a mouse-brown curl falls out of her bonnet and gets stuck to her nose.

'As a matter of fact, she has no time for idle chatter with idle people. We are all very, very busy. The Master and the

Mistress are entertaining and we're short of staff. Catherine can't be spared. Not even for a minute.'

Her face takes on an even redder hue than when she first opened the door, which seems impossible. 'We've a great dinner to prepare and rooms to get ready, so Catherine's a housemaid as well as a kitchen maid today. Nothing I can do about it, mind. You'll have to come back another day.'

Quick, Janet, think!

The door is already closing.

'I understand, and I'm very sorry to have bothered you at a time like this, but…'

The door opens a little again.

'Only Catherine's mother and brother sent fresh cake with her clothes, and it would be a shame to let it spoil by leaving it on the step.' I hold out the basket and at once, I know I did right. The greed in the cook's piggy face is unmistakeable.

'Ach, very well. Pass it here and I'll see that she gets it.' Podgy fingers grasp the basket handle.

'And, I wondered if you needed a hand at all? House or kitchen, I can work hard. I'm only a year younger than Catherine. I wouldn't take much and if it would help… the Schoolmaster in my village is away today.' I stand up straight, hands folded, and try to look trustworthy and modest and industrious and whatever else this woman is looking for.

She looks me up and down. 'Just for today?'

'Just for today is fine.'

'We'd have to clean you up a bit, in case you're seen.' She fingers my stained skirt as if it belonged to her and I have to resist the urge to hit her. Instead I nod in apology.

'But you weren't to know that, lass. We're bound to have a spare uniform somewhere in that linen cupboard.' She turns and walks away, leaving the door wide open. Without a second's hesitation, I follow her inside.

Granna and Mother know I'm here, so they'll think I've been delayed speaking to Catherine. I picture their faces if I come home, not only with news, but with money! Not that it'll be much. I bet it won't be money at all, come to think of it, probably more tokens to spend in Anderson's own swindle-shop by the Rispond Pier. Oh well. So far, so good.

I try to catch Catherine's eye the first time she rushes past me, arms piled high with folded sheets, a cleaning cloth and pail hung from her elbow. It's a wonder she can even see her way up the narrow servant stairs. Stairs are still a bit of a novelty for me, so I eye them from a distance. I'm glad to be down here in the kitchen, peeling potatoes, and I make a good job of it too.

'Not bad at all.' The cook mumbles as she pushes past me. 'Have you helped us out before?'

'Just once.' I concentrate hard on keeping up my speed as I answer, eyes on the work in my hands. 'At Christmas time when Master Anderson had the feast.'

'I wasn't here then.' The cook fetches a ham from the larder.

'I thought I didn't recognise you.' *Keep peeling, Janet...*

'What's your name then?' she asks, sharpening her knife.

'Janet. I'm from Ceannabeinne. Like Catherine. She used to live next door, before she became a maid here. I sometimes look after her brother. He's...'

How am I going to describe Wee Donald? Everyone I've ever spoken to about him has known him all his life, so no need to explain. I peel faster.

'...he needs looking after. A bit.'

Thankfully the woman doesn't seem too interested.

I move on to the cabbage.

CHAPTER EIGHT

Through the Hedge

IT MUST BE AT LEAST ANOTHER HOUR BEFORE CATHERINE reappears. 'Oh Janet! What are you doing here?'

I risk stopping whipping the cream for a minute and allow her to hug me. Her hair has got even blonder over the summer and it's grown, too. I can tell, even though she's got it pinned up in a fancy way, not like at home. She looks older that way, too.

'I'm just helping out. Seems like you've a lot to do.' I grin, whipping the cream so hard that the cook shouts: 'That'll do. That'll do! Thank you!'

Catherine washes her hands and gets ready to take the potatoes off the stove. 'Heaven must have sent you, Janet. I thought I had all this kitchen work to do, so I was running from room to room like a hare in full flight!'

'What else would you like done?' I ask the cook.

'That rubbish there—take it out to the compost heap in

the garden. Up the little steps, behind the house, but make sure you aren't seen. Master Anderson and his guests are about somewhere.'

'Will do.' I can't help it, a wide smile spreads over my face—so much so that Catherine gives me a *what-are-you-up-to-look* and I stand on my own toes to distract myself.

The bucket of potato peel is slimy and I have to hold on tight. Every few steps, I change hands so that the sharp metal handle doesn't cut too deeply. The compost heap is exactly where I expected it to be. However, the voices in the rose garden are much closer than I had dared to hope, almost beside me through the hedge. Granna's fir must be working its luck. I listen hard.

'And that's the best you can do?' *That's Anderson, no mistake.* I've heard him speak before: the growling anger of the old man, a voice used to being obeyed. I almost pity the poor soul at the mercy of his wrath.

'That's what the Superintendent says, Sir, and I don't see any other way myself. He'll travel up tomorrow from Dornoch with the new writ. That'll teach them.'

The Master does not seem impressed. 'But why can't somebody local do it? A local man would be quicker, and I want this blasted business over and done with, do you hear!' He is almost spitting with temper.

'I understand, Sir. The thing is; none of the local men will agree to do it. They feel they're betraying their own. The injured man Campbell is facing eviction himself, I gather, over towards Eriboll.'

My stomach heaves in a wave of guilty nausea.

Anderson just snorts.

'But a figure like the Superintendent, Mr Anderson— think of the effect such a respectable person will have on these rebellious villagers. A proper representative of the law, all the way from the Sheriff Court in Dornoch!'

Again, Anderson is silent and I risk a peek through the hedge into the rose garden where the men are walking. The Master's back is turned, but I can make out a Sheriff Officer uniform on the other man, much like the one Campbell was wearing when he came. I don't recognise him. He speaks again.

'I do feel that someone of a higher rank…'

'VERY WELL,' the Master roars, making me jump backwards. My hand slips on the slimy handle, my feet skid on the greasy ground. I teeter backwards, reaching for anything to stop my fall, but my grasping hands find no grip. Time stands still as I hang in the air, until, both arms flailing, I land in the compost heap with a squelch and my pail clatters to the ground.

I don't move, holding my breath and praying they won't investigate. The silence stretches, giving the damp dung plenty of time to soak into my skirt.

'Let him come,' the Master snaps. 'But take it from me: time is money! The sooner these villages are empty, the sooner the hills are going to be swarming with sheep. Profitable, reliable, hardy sheep.'

Even squinting through the hedge, I can see the white in his eyes. Anderson storms away, followed by the Sheriff Officer who scampers and whimpers after him.

'Janet! Where have you got to?' The cook's voice cuts through the air. My heart plummets once more and I check over my shoulder, wondering if the men could have heard, but they're already halfway down to the main gate by the pier.

'Sorry,' I shout, relieved. 'I found the compost heap at last.'

Running back to the kitchen and rinsing the bucket, the speed of my brain dizzies me as it tries to make sense of it all.

Tomorrow.

Superintendent from Dornoch. And then, most terribly of all…

New Writ.

'Look at the state of you, lass! Catherine, you will need to lend Janet some fresh clothes. And here, take the bundle upstairs with you, will you?'

No mention or trace of the cake, as I suspected. Still, neither of us need to be told twice—we haven't had a break all day.

As soon as we are on our own, the whole thing seems even more dreadful than before. I think about how to break it to Catherine, but her face is already grim.

'I know all about Ceannabeinne, Janet. I heard yesterday, after the Master had the visitor.'

I think of the man Campbell, his shirt in shreds, his arm burnt. And to think, the same is happening to *his* village…

'Nasty blister you've got there, Janet.' She looks at me solemnly, but then the corners of her mouth edge upwards. 'You really showed him, didn't you?'

I break into a half-hearted grin. My blisters sting, but Campbell's are bound to sting more.

'I am worried nothing good will come of it, Janet. The Master was beside himself last night. He hardly touched his dinner, the footman said.'

My whole body gives a shiver. I doubt I'm going to have much of an appetite either, after what I've heard today.

How on earth are any of us going to sleep tonight?

CHAPTER NINE

Battle Lines

ON ANY OTHER DAY, SPENT PEELING AND SCRUBBING AND folding and running errands for a single meagre token, I'd have crawled home, slow as a slug.

But tonight, it's as if the clear air opens my lungs. I sprint over the smooth Rispond road. I don't think about who may be lying in wait by the dark lochans, nor do I cast a single glance at the dark crevices that normally stir my imagination to a frenzy. I run up above the cliffs, as the waves cheer me on below. I barely break sweat until I reach the schoolhouse, where the Schoolmaster's weedy figure briefly casts a shadow against the curtains. Nosy man!

Past the Big Boulder. Down towards Ceannabeinne and the sea, the faint lights of Smoo and Sangomore flicker against the darkening sky. If anything, my strides lengthen. There may be little light now, but I know every pebble of this path. I make up my mind and continue full pelt past my home and up the narrow wind to Hugh Munro's cottage. I'm sure more than one door opens in response to my fraught knocks. Hugh greets me just as Father or Angus would.

'Janet.'

I didn't realise how out of breath I was until I sit down. Thankfully, Hugh has sent Wee Donald round the houses for all the men to come, immediately. Father is one of the first to appear. He gives me a long, long look and takes his stand by the window, pulling the curtain back to watch the arrivals, slowly stroking his beard. Hugh pulls the heavy fabric across.

'Let's keep the gale out, please. The wife is hardly going to get better if we invite the weather right in.'

It is getting colder, right enough; even I notice it. I drop to my knees and tend Hugh and Margaret's fire while everyone gathers around it and me, brown smoke obscuring their dour faces. The room is full to bursting, and I'm the only female, if you don't count a hen in the corner by the door. Even Margaret Munro has gathered her knitting and blankets and has taken them to the Seamstress's house next door.

'So, we'd better hear what Janet has to say. Go on, Janet!' Hugh's voice is deep and calm, and behind him, Father nods his approval. Hugh winks and it feels as if it's only the three of us in the room as my words tumble over one another like pebbles in the surf.

The next morning, Father and the rest of the men who work at the Rispond Estate leave earlier than usual. Father rubs my shoulder as he passes me, and he stops to put his hands on either side of Mother's face.

'Be brave, lass. We'll be here on time. Come, Angus.'

I watch them disappear and take the pot and the griddle to the burn. Peggy from the Top House is already there.

'How are you, Peggy?' I sigh.

'Is it true?' Her voice is even sharper than usual. She raises herself to her full height and turns her face at an angle so I have a chance to appreciate the elegant twists in her hair. No doubt she practised that move in front of the looking glass.

'Is it true, Janet, that you are stirring up a rebellion? Because it's not godly, you know? Father says he is on excellent terms with Mr Anderson and that it would be a mistake to offend the Master in any way.'

I don't know what it is, but something snaps, like a reed twisted too dry and too hard. I swing the full pot of old tea and peaty burn water and I hurl it at her.

It's as if time has frozen. She makes no sound at all. I

stare, astounded as brown water drips from each shaggy strand of hair. Tea leaves are sticking to her cheeks and on her teeth. Her dress, floating in the wind before, hangs down heavy and wet.

The bubbling begins, deep within me at first. I thought I'd want to laugh, but it's anger that boils, as if the devil himself stood before me, dripping by the burn.

'Peggy, are you really so simple that Wee Donald understands it and you don't? No-one will get to stay. *No-one*, do you hear? And you—in your fancy Top House—with the most to lose of us all! How would you like to see your precious gable chimneys crumble, huh? How would you like the fancy glass windows smashed, and your fancy smooth floors and... and... your nice thick chain for the pot ripped down, thrown out and trampled into the mud; and whatever else they can think of to do?'

I am screaming, but I don't care who hears me now. The worst part is that I can feel it start: the tears are going to come and Peggy Mackay from the Top House is going to see me cry, and that's got to be even worse than anything else that's already happened. I don't let it stop me.

'And we may not stand a chance because your father's honourable Master Anderson has not even listened to the man of God! Yes, Peggy, we're going to try—those of us who have a bit of pride and a bit of courage. But that's all right, Peggy, you just hide in your comfortable fancy Top House and admire how pretty you are in the looking glass until THE WALLS COME DOWN AROUND YOU and you're sent away to Lord knows where and even your precious Daddy and his excellent terms with Master Anderson won't make a difference, all because YOU ARE NOT SHEEP!'

I feel faint, so I take a deep breath, and the tears come. Peggy turns, gathers her things and walks stiffly up the path —until I can't see her clearly anymore.

I'm still sitting by the burn, asking the Lord for forgiveness, when I hear the creaks of Isabella's cart.

It's a miracle she can pull that thing at all with her spindly legs. It's even harder to imagine her pulling it all the way to the hill cave where the two are going to hide out for the time being. The Seamstress emerges from her own house with a bundle.

'Ready?'

'I suppose.' The Seamstress's face looks taut, like a sail about to tear in an invisible storm.

'Farewell, Janet. We will see you soon.'

Isabella *knows*. I don't know how, but she knows all about the worry-storm in my mind, and her one squeeze of my shoulder makes it better.

Not all right.

But *better*.

As the shapes of the two women disappear towards the schoolhouse, along the Durine Road and then up into the hills, I think of another person, making a journey at this very moment.

His title itself tastes of fear: Superintendent of Dornoch.

I snap into action, remembering all that I was supposed to do while Father and Angus were away. The things Hugh Munro told me to see to. How long have I been sitting here idle while evil oozes up from Dornoch, mile, by mile, by mile? Will he have a horse? He is bound to have a horse. He could be here in the afternoon, if he changes horses at Altnaharra. Not much time at all.

I give the pot and griddle a quick rinse and pelt back to the house as if my skirt was on fire.

The pile of stones behind the outbuildings is growing by the minute as every woman and child brings apronful after apronful. The sun has come out and Ceannabeinne is bathed in the lovely autumn glow that simply doesn't allow misery. I'm ashamed when I think of this morning; letting Peggy get the better of me and allowing fear to take hold.

It must be true what the Reverend says: *perfect love driveth out fear*. We are in this together, more than we ever were before. And isn't this love: everyone giving their all, so that Isabella's and the Seamstress's sacrifice isn't for nothing?

Looking back down at the rocky armoury at my feet, I'm not too sure whether this is the kind of love the Reverend had in mind.

Little William has been sent to the Big Boulder to keep watch. He's the best at the loud whistling, and the first signal rings out now: two low whistles followed by one high.

'Our men are coming back!'

Relief ripples through our crowd, especially as there's no sign of the unwelcome visitor yet.

'R-ready, Janet?' Wee Donald has come up to join me.

'Donald! What on earth is that?'

Wee Donald stares down at the chanter in his hand. As do I. However hard I try, his reason for bringing a musical instrument out here, now of all times, is *not* obvious to me. I try again.

'What I meant was, why have you brought your chanter out? Especially right now, when there's so much else to do?'

'Do you mean when we're trying to fight off the n-nasty man who wants us off the l-land?'

I sigh. If only everyone spoke as plainly as that. Life

would be simpler. 'Yes.'

'Hugh s-said to bring it. He's bringing his b-bagpipes, too.' He shrugs.

I nearly drop the stones I'm stacking. 'Really?'

'Yes. He says that a bit of f-fierce music might be as scary as stones.'

The men are beginning to appear and before long, almost the whole village is gathered by the burn, apart from the Schoolmaster who "wants no part in this folly", and little William who is keeping watch by the Big Boulder. There's no sign of the Top House Mackays.

Father and Hugh Munro look up at the road and Father squints like he does when he's thinking. 'Best to have a bite outside. I daren't go in, for fear of missing the signal. Angus, go up to take over from William. The lad's done well, but he's been there for hours.'

Angus rolls his eyes behind Father's back, but he obeys and minutes later, William joins us for stew and bread.

'You've done well, William. Good lad.' Hugh offers him a pat on the back, but his hand is stilled in mid-air. 'What's this?'

All our eyes follow his up the path, where Mr Mackay stomps down from the Top House. He casts a sideways glance at the stones we've stacked and shakes his head. His wife and Peggy follow, with Hector lingering behind.

'Hugh.'

'How can I help you, George Mackay?' *Oh dear, I've not heard Hugh like this before.* There's a seething beneath his civility. It's as if no-one breathes.

The Top House Mackays look serious and Mr George Mackay speaks with blistering bitterness:

'I don't know what you think you're going to achieve, but I'd advise you to think again.' He's addressing all of us now.

'I've watched you since getting back, and Mrs Mackay here has observed for most of the day. There's a barbarity here. Even the girls... '

His eyes bore into mine now and I glance at Peggy, spotless as usual. My own eyes travel down from my frayed collar to my peat-stained apron and the scratched hands that have handled a thousand rocks in the last few hours.

Peggy's father is not finished yet. 'Do you all really think the Master is going to keep paying wages to a bunch of troublemakers? And what will you do without the fishing work out of Rispond, eh? What would I do? Who else would employ a boat builder? If I can't work in Rispond, what could I do?'

Hugh breathes deeply. 'We've been on this land for generations, some of us. Others came to flee the evil of the

Clearances elsewhere. We have worked hard for Anderson, and we deserve better than to be handed a writ and be turned out of our homes a couple of days later. Now, choose! You can help us, or you can hide.'

Hugh looks at all of us over his shoulder and raises his eyebrows.

'No. I'll not do either of that.' Mackay hesitates for a second before continuing.

'In fact, I'll go and warn the gentleman from Dornoch of the outrage you're planning.' He turns and starts to walk up the path again, but my mother, of all people, has grabbed his elbow. He lifts his fist. Surely he's not going to strike a woman? I fly at his raised arm at the same time as Father and before I know it, Mrs Mackay and Peggy are shrieking. Hector appears from somewhere and shouts to let go, and Hugh's mouth is moving, but I can't make a thing out in this din. Something catches the corner of my vision. The world is moving and shifting. Even as I'm being tugged this way and that, I sense that *something* is wrong; even more wrong than the way we're thrashing and clawing and yelling at one another.

And finally, it sinks in.

It's Angus, crashing down the hillside, shouting at the top of his voice. Which can only mean one thing.

It's time.

Strathnaver 1814: The Mob

Anna's husband sprang to his feet like a bird flutters in panic. The hoof beats thudded on the Altnaharra Road—not one horse, not two. No, more than Anna had ever heard at any one time, a steady whinnying drumbeat, turning the rush of the stream into a battle march.

The villagers stood outside every house, watching as the procession of riders drew near. All of them carried torches in their hands, apart from the Factor himself.

Then, Sellar's sharp voice travelled on the wind. 'You should be gone. Be gone!'

'We have nowhere to go. This is our home,' John shouted. A hundred people's anger and fear filled the glen.

Anna could feel it.

CHAPTER TEN

The Mackintosh Coat

IT'S LIKE A MAGICAL BREEZE, RELEASING US FROM AN EVIL SPELL. I loosen my hold on Mr Mackay, dropping my hands. Peggy lets go of my hair and Mother and Mrs Mackay dust themselves down. All our faces turn to Angus, careering towards us. His face is flushed.

'I whistled the signal! I whistled the signal, again and again! What in the name of Heaven were you doing?'

'No need for that language, son', grumbles Father and I nearly smirk, seeing as he's only just stopped hurling insults at the Top House Mackays for threatening Mother.

Angus can barely breathe, but he's shouting regardless. 'He's here! Don't you see? He's coming...', my brother gasps, 'NOW! He'll be passing the schoolhouse any moment!'

Right enough, a lone rider has appeared on the road high above us. My heart stops, but the waves carry on slapping down on the beach, as if nothing was wrong at all.

Mr Mackay steps forward, but Hugh thunders: 'Stay back, George! He can thrust the writ into your hands, and that'll be it. Stay back, everyone!'

The man is not even within throwing distance yet, but we all recoil like he had the plague. Peggy inadvertently steps into the burn backwards, I notice with satisfaction.

'*Feasgar math*!' yells Hugh, from a distance. Whatever happens next, the polite Gaelic greeting must be observed. 'How are you today?' Hugh walks forward, his white hair whipped by the wind.

'Good evening to you too,' the Superintendent responds, cautiously. I elbow my way past Angus and Hector to get a better view. He's wearing a fashionable coat and a hat. His horse, however, looks worse than the old mare after a day's ploughing and I have to resist the urge to run towards it with a bucket of water. I wonder if the beast has had a single kind pat all day. *Is the Superintendent from Dornoch such a man, the sort who pats a horse?*

As if in answer, he uses a whip to urge it forward onto the uneven path. He passes the Top House, digging his spurs into the animal's belly, but it nearly stumbles. 'It's bleeding,' Hector Mackay whispers into my ear from behind. 'See it, Janet? His horse is bleeding where he kicks the spurs in.'

The man gives up and dismounts, taking a rolled paper

from the saddle bag.

'Sir, may we be so free as to ask what business you have here?' Hugh's voice carries on the wind. The man has thrown the horse's reins over the trough by the outhouse. His voice, the English, sounds nasal and dry when it comes, not at all like the song of the land that chimes with all our Gaelic speech.

'I'll make this brief. A most disturbing account of disobedience has reached headquarters, which made it necessary for me to take the troublesome journey from Dornoch upon myself. But that nonsense will have to stop here, by the power of the law. By the authority invested in me…'

'Stop!' Hugh calls out.

The high-ranking visitor clearly didn't expect to be interrupted, but he falls silent in the face of Hugh's authority. I'm close enough now to see the shine of sweat on the man's forehead and he takes his expensive Mackintosh coat off, slinging it over his shoulder. Again, Hugh walks forward.

'Listen to me. I respect your authority and your position. Please, would you make clear to a simple man what plans the honourable Master Anderson has for our village? We'll be reasonable, I promise you that.'

The Superintendent seems heartened by these words and

takes another step towards us. I eye the paper suspiciously. Hugh's voice is calm, almost disinterested, when he speaks.

'Is it Master Anderson's intention that we leave the land, days from now, never to return?'

'I'm afraid so. The Master holds the lease and can do as he pleases. This is not news to you. I know it will cause you some difficulty, but one must submit to the law—or suffer the consequences.'

The Superintendent's tone has become edgier, but our elder remains unruffled. Looking straight at Mackay from the Top House, Hugh asks: 'And does this mean that *all* the houses here are to be demolished?'

'Master Anderson will turn all of this estate into sheep farming, yes. As I understand it, only the schoolhouse will remain as housing for the shepherds from England. But that is neither here nor there. He has the authority to remove you and he has chosen to do so now.'

Hugh has not taken his eyes off the Top House people. 'Even the boatbuilding will cease?'

'Yes. All current business will be replaced by sheep farming; it's a decision your Master Anderson is perfectly entitled to make. He now claims back all land for this purpose.' The Superintendent steps forward. 'Now, I've been truthful with you. As you've agreed to be reasonable, it is your legal obligation to receive this writ which details…'

But what exactly it details, we never find out, for Hugh has given the sign. The first stone, flung by Wee Donald, lands inches from the important gentleman's feet. Hugh's voice roars above our cheers.

'It is a *reasonable* response to a cruel unkindness. Seems like it's raining rocks, Sir.'

I join Wee Donald, and my rock makes contact with the Superintendent's shin. He winces.

Hugh gives a bitter laugh. 'It'll get heavy, I fear. Uncanny. Highland weather; there's nothing like it.'

To my surprise, the first adult to join in is Mr Mackay from the Top House, throwing a handful of stones at once.

'The horse! Don't hit the horse!' Hector shouts and I aim carefully, letting my rock splash into the trough. As I hoped, the animal shies and rears. The reins snap and it runs off up the hill and into the moorland towards Rispond. If the man has noticed, he doesn't show it, cursing as he dances backwards to avoid the stones. We advance on him, step by step, throw by throw, and when Hugh and Wee Donald strike up the tune *Caberfeidh* on their bagpipes, we cheer and throw in time with the music as the stranger scrambles up the path and retreats, shouting after his horse. The writ is still clutched in his hand as he turns the corner into

Rispond and I tear after him. Angus catches me up easily. 'He's gone,' he pants. 'What are you doing?'

'Don't worry, I'm not going far. Just to take the saddle and bridle off the poor beast.'

He nods and drops back.

High on the outcrop above Anderson's estate, I manage to catch the terrified mare. Soon, the saddle and blanket lie on the rocks near the road and the animal calms down a little, nostrils flaring.

Angus arrives a few minutes later with a pail of water. I guess he's not all bad, even though he's my brother. We take care to stay well out of sight as we rub down her coat and slap her on the rear to send her towards the Rispond stables.

On the way back, my feet get caught in something and Angus has to steady me before I fall.

A smile spreads across his face.

'Look what we found!' announces Angus, as we rejoin the others.

The Superintendent's posh Mackintosh coat is raised high on a pole like a flag as music rings out into the night sky and the story is told again and again. The tune *Caberfeidh* concludes our feast and every lass and woman dances with every lad and man before the night is out. Mr Mackay from the Top House must have had more than a few drams, for his fiddle's fury possesses the air like never before. Granna strokes the cat on her lap as I sing.

Life is good.

For now.

CHAPTER ELEVEN

The First Reckoning

GRANNA KNEELS BY HER BED LONGER THAN USUAL THE next morning. The Schoolmaster is back, so there are no more excuses; I'll simply have to bear him. With a sigh, I stack more peat onto the fire to make a brew.

Sometimes I wonder why the Schoolmaster's taken against me quite so harshly, but then why should he care for me when I think of *him* as the devil incarnate? Hector doesn't mind him much. But then, Hector is from the Top House, and the Schoolmaster is just the type to be impressed by gable chimneys and glass windows and plastered walls and such things. Come to think of it, for a Top House Mackay, Hector's not so bad. Peggy is a different matter.

Granna is still on her knees, her low prayer accompanied by the wind whistling through the cracks between the stones. I bet there's none of that in the Top House. The draught, I mean. Mind, I don't know how much praying goes on there either.

I see it all before my eyes again, Mr and Mrs Mackay joining in the shouts and hurling stones to scare the Dornoch man away. His face! And he deserved it all, no doubt about that, especially the way he treated his poor horse. A new wave of victory joy washes over me and I can't help it, I begin to hum the *Caberfeidh* tune as I dust the flour off the griddle. As if in protest, Granna's prayer gets louder.

I hum on, thinking of last night: the pats on the back from everyone, Angus running up to the hill cave to tell Isabella and the Seamstress, the way they risked it for the evening and came down to join us for music and stories.

'*Amen!*' Granna shouts, and leans against the box bed to push herself upright.

I give her a radiant smile which she doesn't return.

'Aren't you even a little bit pleased, Granna? We stood our ground, didn't we? Mind how Hugh Munro spoke to the man? He was making fun of him and he couldn't get near us with that writ, could he Granna?'

My grandmother has already wandered off, fingering the pot chain and crumbling a charred pine needle between her fingers.

'Granna, what is it?'

She shakes her head, which annoys me. *Why can't she just tell me?*

'Anyway, I have to go to the schoolhouse. I can't be late, or else the Schoolmaster will...'

I don't even know what the Schoolmaster will do. Throw me out of school? I'd thank him gladly and tend cattle and fields all day! And because I can't think of a good way to finish the sentence, I don't bother at all. Taking the old satchel that was Angus's before me, I run up the hill, waving to Mother who's already harvesting cabbages.

But when I pass the Big Boulder, I nearly stumble. There are figures, slowly edging up the Rispond road, not like an army, no, not like that at all.

Like a funeral procession. With Father at the head.

The Schoolmaster rings the bell and I have no choice: I know he's looking at me as always, trying to find a reason to scold me. I make sure I'm second in line to go in, and clean the board for good measure. Strange: he doesn't seem remotely interested. Instead, he is looking out of the window, narrowing his eyes.

It takes all of us sitting silently for prayer to snap him out of his day-dream.

'Good morning children.'

'Good morning, Mr Muir,' we chant, half-heartedly.

'Let us pray.' Still, his eyes dance to the window.

'Our Father, who art in heaven, hallowed be thy name...'

All of us chorus along of course, but I open my eyes for a moment and, through the window, see the top of the men's heads returning from Rispond. Father's face is grim, Angus's flushed with anger. Mr Mackay from the Top House looks simply defeated.

I can't risk being caught by the Schoolmaster, so I redouble my efforts. 'For thine is the kingdom, the power and the glory, for ever and ever. Amen.'

His eyes are narrow, and on me alone.

I can barely think straight during the arithmetic lesson.

At lunchtime, I make for the door and nearly bump into the messenger bringing the papers, a few days out of date, but still. He is holding the *Inverness Courier* in his hands.

'Morning all. You'd never guess—Ceannabeinne is famous, Sir. Would you pass this on to the village elder, please?' The messenger grins, but none of us grin back. Still, he stands in the doorway. I wish I could get past. I long to run home and see about Father and Angus and the others. *Why have they come home? The weather is fair, so surely the boats could have gone out?* It's all wrong and I can't think of anything that'll make it right.

My eyes catch the headline and inadvertently, my hands are drawn to the paper. *'Uncouth Highlanders Assault Servant of the Law'.*

How could news of this have reached Inverness already? It's dated before... Oh, it must refer to the first writ and that Mr Campbell.

'May I see, Sir? Please? I could take it down to Hugh Munro, I'm running back to the village anyway.'

'Give me that, and be on your way, silly girl,' spits the Schoolmaster, ripping the newspaper out of my hand. His mouth creeps up into a smile as he mumbles snippets under his breath. *'Ill-informed revolt... Landlord's legal right to... Infamous local leader Hugh Munro...* hahaha... *Serious consequences... Dornoch officials to get involved...* ha. They should have listened to me, shouldn't they?'

I've heard enough. Slamming the door behind me, I race down the hill, along the path and burst into our house. I blink, willing my eyes to adjust to the dim light, and see Father and Angus seated by the hearth. *Father, smoking a pipe before sunset? It is simply unheard of!* His face is drawn.

'What news?' is all I can wheeze.

Father averts his eyes and stokes the fire, but Mother paces towards me and throws her arms around me. Angus rises before he speaks.

'The Master Anderson has decided he does not need the workers from Ceannabeinne anymore.'

It makes such sense that I cannot believe I didn't expect it.

'He sent us all home. When old Harrison of Durine spoke up for us, he was told not to come back either. There'll be no more work for us in Rispond. Or for any who help us.'

'But…' There is too much in my heart to say. *It's as wrong as wrong can be; it goes against all the good Lord teaches! Will we be forced to abandon this land, this house which my father's father built before he was lost at sea—the grandfather I never met? And will Granna be turned out of her home all over again?* It is this thought which steels my resolve.

'There's more,' I whisper. They deserve to know.

Even my father raises his face to me at that.

'The newspaper arrived from Inverness. The Schoolmaster has it. I offered to take it to the village but he wouldn't let me, despicable man!'

'Janet!' cautions Granna, and Father gives me a disapproving stare.

'Oh, very well; I shouldn't speak of him like this, but he brings it on himself. And I know neither of you like him either!'

'What about the paper? Do you know what it said?' Father's voice is gentle.

'I'm afraid it's not good news for us, Father.' And I try my best, repeating word for word what I saw and read and what the Schoolmaster said. When I finally finish, Father breaks the silence, already rising from his chair.

'I never thought that one day I'd be glad I have a daughter who can read. Well done, Janet. You have proved your worth today. As for everything else, we'll have to trust the Lord to provide. I'll go to see the Reverend Finlayson, but I'll have to call on Hugh on the way. I may not be back until nightfall.'

He doesn't even stop to finish his pipe or take provisions. His determined strides echo out on the stones. I picture the scene in every house. Working men and lads sitting by the fire in the middle of the day: defeated; desperate; fearful; helpless. Useless in the face of this evil power.

I jump when the school bell rings again for afternoon lessons. Now I'll be late for certain, and I'll get a beating for it.

No doubt whatever about that!

Chapter Twelve

The Return

The afternoon walk back to the village takes me ten times as long with the pain. It seems that Angus's old satchel has quadrupled in weight.

I always wonder where the Schoolmaster summons the strength, him such a weak-looking man. When he hits me with that leather tawse, he becomes properly possessed. I can barely bend my knuckles without breaking the fresh scabs and Peggy's spiteful laughter still rings in my ears. My back aches from the caning that went before and I distract myself by inventing suitable punishments for Mr Muir, like hanging and drawing and quartering and feeding him to the crows.

By the time I reach the path to the village, I begin to wonder for real. *Could our men be arrested for defending their homes?*

Locked up?

Or even killed?

87

Could they?

I imagine Father walking towards a noose; I see Granna standing beside him and resolve to stop thinking at all. I hate where my mind takes me at times. Instead, I decide to do something good for the Seamstress and Isabella, still hidden in the cave high above the village. A thin plume of smoke is the only giveaway. There are wild brambles in Durine. Maybe I can go to collect some for them…

'Janet!'

I swing round. I thought I was the last one home. All the younger children went ahead, and Peggy wouldn't walk with me if her life depended on it. Maybe she is a little scared of me at last. Although she threatened me this morning: 'You wait, Janet! I'll pay you back, and not in a way you'll expect!'

She'll forget, so I just laughed in her face. Mind; that was before the Schoolmaster's beating.

'Janet! Wait for me!'

It's Catherine behind me on the path, running towards me.

This, too, feels wrong, but then nothing feels right anymore.

She is out of breath when she reaches me, and no wonder, looking at the size of her bundle. It seems she is carrying the whole of the Rispond household on her back.

'I thought that was you, Janet. Are you hurt? You're moving like…'

'A lame partan crab? Yes, that sounds about right!'

We both laugh, but it's a sad laugh and both of us know it.

'They've let me go, Janet.'

'What? But you weren't even here when it all happened.'

'I'm a risk. They're worried I'll spy. It's my village causing the trouble, isn't it?'

Guilt cuts through me, more painful than my swollen hands.

'Will he take you back? In the future, I mean?'

'Oh, Janet, I don't know. I hardly know anything anymore.'

Last week, the future meant forever. The future meant the land. It meant the cool stone of our longhouse, the cat by the hearth, the yard, the hills and the cattle.

'What is the Master going to do now? Did you hear anything, Catherine? Do you think he'll give in?'

She shakes her head. 'The Master doesn't give in, Janet; not ever. I heard the Superintendent last night, and he was even angrier than Master Anderson. He's off to Dornoch again, but I fear…'

'What?'

'He said something about raising a trusty party.'

I spin round to look at my friend. 'Trusty party? What in the world is that?'

'I didn't know either, so I asked the cook. It sounds like he'll make his way up from Dornoch, and he'll ask people to fight for him on the way, you know. He'll pay them; however many are willing. Oh Janet, what if he finds a lot? It's not as if our fathers are fighters, and these men could be thugs and ruffians and the like!'

I don't know what to say. Instead, I start limping forward again, past the Top House where Peggy is watching from the window. Does she never have anything better to do? By the burn, Catherine is nearly knocked over by Wee Donald, throwing himself at his sister in a fierce hug.

Moments later, we arrive at Hugh Munro's house. Let him worry about what to do. He'll know a way.

He has to.

Inch by inch, I creak onto the low chair and wince. Mrs Munro does look tired, but she's on her feet, frowning down at me.

'What's wrong, lass?'

'I took a beating at school.'

I try to sit up straight, so my coat hides my throbbing hands, but too late: the blood-encrusted knuckles speak for themselves.

'Hugh, I think you need to have a word with the Schoolmaster, dear. Would you look at Janet's hands!'

I shift uncomfortably. 'No, it's nothing! Nothing at all. Listen to Catherine. She's got more news.'

Hugh stokes the flames and sits, his white hair alive with gold and amber as he leans over the fire. His eyes still sparkle. He doesn't interrupt once, only listens and nods and smiles his encouragement when Catherine is lost for words, until she is finished.

Mrs Munro brings us warm milk and honey, the peat glimmers and Hugh speaks words of comfort. Despite all that is happening, I feel safe; as if the Schoolmaster and Master Anderson and the Superintendent from Dornoch were all just spirits in the night. Wee Donald appears and clings to his sister like he can't believe she is actually back, and by the time I return to the house, feed the cattle and start the broth for supper, my strength and my resolve are making a slow return.

Before long, I'm hatching a plan.

Chapter Thirteen

The Plan

THE MORE I THINK ABOUT IT, THE MORE EXCITED I GET. But I can't tell Father or Mother or anyone. Again, I count out in my head all the rules I'm going to break and I wonder if the Minister would approve. But he preached about being cunning as foxes, and if ever there was a time to be cunning, then surely it's now.

I bite my lip, hard, else I may fall asleep. Mother and Father are breathing deeply, but I'm not so sure about Angus. I lie still until I get pins and needles in my feet. Angus snores, always, but he's not snoring now.

There's no point in going much before sunrise, I calculate. Again, I try to imagine myself in the Superintendent's shoes, and I picture him at the helm of a huge army of ruffians, heading towards me with determined steps, like a dance. I can hear the drum, keeping rhythm as they advance. Right, boom, boom, left, boom, boom, right, boom, boom, left...

Some noise startles me and I bite my lip again, this time in annoyance that I allowed myself to fall asleep. With the tiniest of careful movements, I peek up at the cloth covering the small window. The horizon is already turning pink; I can tell by the edges. No time to lose. I push the blanket off and silently pull on my pinafore and my apron, never taking my eye off my sleeping parents. When I reach for the woollen shawl, I feel a hand on my shoulder.

Angus puts his finger to his lips and motions outside. I must have woken him. *Oh no, this will only complicate things...* Silently, we tiptoe out into the dawn, the air thick with haar from the sea. *Why isn't he giving me away?* Neither of us speak at all until we reach the field where the young village mare grazes in the late moon, barely an outline. No-one will hear us here, but we still lean close and whisper.

'Angus...'

'I'm coming with you.'

'What?' That definitely was not what I was expecting. 'What do you mean, Angus? I'm not going anywhere.'

'Of course not,' he winks, offering the mare a carrot and sliding the bridle from the shelter over her head.

'Just as well we keep all tack in the outhouse here. Were you planning to ride bareback, Janet?'

I nod, before I realise that it's the admission he was

looking for.

I groan. 'All right, fine! I *am* going somewhere and I was planning to use the mare, but I'll bring her back, and I'll be careful, I promise! I'm not going far—well, not *that* far.'

He offers me his clasped hands as a step and I climb onto the mare's back. She rears a little, but it's easy enough to get her back under control. 'I'll open the gate for you,' my brother says, climbing up the fence and loosening the rope. I didn't expect that either, and all without questions. But when I pass through the gate, he suddenly jumps on the mare's back behind me. I can't help giving a little startled cry, but even if anyone heard, we'll not be around long for them to find us. Angus digs his heels in and the faithful horse begins to trot towards the road.

'Bareback is definitely best,' he whispers in my ear. 'There wouldn't be room for me otherwise!'

We reach the road and slow the horse again. It's quieter that way. I swear I see a curtain ripple at the schoolhouse, but no use worrying about that now. As soon as we reach the corner, it's only the cliffs, the sea and us. I turn as far as I'm able, with the mare moving and Angus holding on.

'Angus, go back. Really. I'm not even sure it'll work!'

'Oh we'll make it work. And a good plan it is too!'

I elbow backwards, but he just laughs.

'Seriously, Angus! You don't even know what my plan is.'

'Oh, I think I have a fair idea. You're planning to go to the Eriboll ferry and, somehow, stop that trusty party. After all, they have to come that way.'

I'm actually speechless.

'Am I right?'

I stare straight ahead, mainly because I don't want to answer.

'Am I?' He pokes my ribs and I laugh.

'Very well, yes then. That's what I thought of, but I've still to figure out…'

The sun greets us over the hill. 'Tell me on the way,' says Angus and he kicks the mare into a canter.

By mid-morning, I'm really regretting not leaving a note. I'm always like that; worrying what people think, fretting over disappointing Mother or Father or Granna or Hugh or Mary, or Wee Donald.

Especially Wee Donald.

Angus is the opposite. Once he has made his mind up, he doesn't waver or worry. I'm jealous, for I can't help myself right now. Doubts seep into my heart like water into sand, and before long, it's worry-logged.

We ride through the windswept settlements; pass

scattered buildings one by one, see women in the distance, working their barren runrigs on this rocky coast. The fertile Strathnaver glen where most of our people came from—Granna and her husband among them—is almost legend.

Again, I think of the plan. I must play my part. Even though no soul but the good Lord can hear us, Angus and I whisper, agreeing our performance to the minutest detail as the ferry port comes into view. The boat is anchored. So far, no sign of the ferryman.

'Are you sure he'll agree to it, Angus? And could it work?'

'He'll remember we've an aunt in Laid; we've passed through often enough.' Angus jumps off and leads the horse by the reins. 'All we can do is try.'

Angus doesn't look back as he leads the thirsty mare down towards the ferry pier. I follow a few paces behind. From a distance, the ferryman will think we are his first paying passengers across Loch Eriboll this morning. He'll be disappointed.

It shows on his face.

He emerges from the cottage, eager and alert, but his smile drops with the recognition—he knows our faces. Besides, our ragged clothes put beyond doubt that we don't have money for the fare. And what would two youngsters travel across Loch Eriboll for anyway?

Slowly, suspicion slithers across his weathered features. 'Madainn mhath.'

The ferryman's Gaelic 'good morning' feels empty, and he doesn't wait for an answer. 'You know where the spring is. Water your horse.'

The ferryman doesn't address me, of course, just Angus—almost a young man and nearly worth speaking to. This gives me a chance to look at him more closely than I ever have.

He must be older than Father, with his white-scratched beard and stern stare. He looks like the survivor he is, crossing the deadly Loch Eriboll twice or more a day since he was a boy. His wife, a rod-straight, thin woman, is nowhere to be seen, but I saw her once at my aunt's village. The good Lord never did give them children, as far as I know.

He turns, takes a telescope from a hook by the door and walks to the water's edge to peer across to the opposite shore.

Angus glances at me, frustrated. His freckles stand out against his paling skin.

'What now, Janet?'

'You're asking me?'

'I suppose I am. You had the idea.'

My temper flares. 'We'll have to try again,' I hiss.

'Try what?' A sneering voice behind us makes me jump.

Both of us wheel round and there she is, Mrs Straight-back Tight-bun: the ferryman's wife. Now my brother looks really helpless. And the ghosts of my short lifetime of sermons drift through my mind: *no spirit of fear... be strong and courageous...*

I decide to risk it all and tell this woman the truth. To hand her the power to undo it all. Angus can only shake his head and sink to the ground where the mare grazes.

'Erm… how are you today?'

She nods, pleased with my politeness.

'My good lady, I will tell you the truth, but I beg you not to give us away. We are from Ceannabeinne, over on the other side of the Rispond Estate. They told our village to…'

The woman nods and I see that the ferryman has also approached, his features still.

'We know about Ceannabeinne,' he interrupts.

What does that mean?

While I puzzle, the ferryman offers his explanation: 'The man Campbell—the Sheriff Officer who served the writ…'

My stomach clenches at the memory.

'You lot gave Campbell a hard time, I hear. He's not a bad sort, really, and only the messenger. Master Anderson is turning Port Chamuil out, too, right here. All of us.

Campbell just stays up the field there.'

There it is again, the groundswell of guilt, stronger and fiercer than before: this is bigger, much bigger, than our village alone.

All the more reason to try, I decide. 'I was there, Sir, and we meant him no harm. I'm sorry to hear about this place, too. It's a great wrong and we must at least try to stop it. We have refused the writ, twice now, even though the papers in Inverness are reporting it all. Did you see?'

The man and the woman nod. I wonder if the ferry port will remain. *I suppose even shepherds need to travel, do they not?*

'But what's your struggle got to do with us?' the woman demands, impatient now.

Angus tells them of my plan and the trusty party, bound to arrive on the opposite shore anytime today and requiring passage. If only we could join the ferry and plant our tale. If only the ferryman were kind enough to accept us as passengers, or helpers, or both. If only he agreed, out of kindness and mercy, as a service to the Lord, to take no payment.

For we have none.

We wait for his answer and the seconds stretch. The ferryman has lifted his telescope to his eye again and peers across to the other side of the Loch.

'There are people waiting on the other side. We'd better go. Come.'

His wife smiles encouragement and we walk after him as quickly as we can, before he changes his mind.

Chapter Fourteen

The Trusty Party

OUR HORSE LOOKS LIKE A MERE TOY FROM SUCH A DISTANCE. I reach down to the water, follow its flow to the ocean with my eyes and look away, fearful of the thousands of lives claimed by its unknown depths. Of Granna's husband John, the grandfather I never met, and all the others: Mary's husband; Isabella's nephew too; the two brothers from the island, only last year.

There is a shrieking kind of silence here, nothing but gulls, reminding us that we are intruders.

The ferryman doesn't speak beyond instructions, mainly for Angus—who is keen to make himself as useful as possible—and he doesn't do too badly. There is a shadow of an approving smile at least once, when Angus moves the rudder to avoid a drifting log.

Soon, the grazing mare is but a dot on the heath and the opposite pier comes into sharp focus. I narrow my eyes.

Oh Lord! No!

I scramble across the deck to Angus and lean in to shout into his ear over the wind.

'It's him! He's here again!'

Angus takes a second to work out who I mean, but then his eyes widen. 'He won't recognise us, Janet, will he? There were so many of us after all, and he would have been more concerned with stones flying at him than memorising faces, surely?'

I don't have time to glory in the fact that my brother actually asked my opinion. With lightning speed, I cast about for ways to disguise my appearance. My sweaty hands pleat my unruly hair and tuck it into my coat and I wrap a woollen blanket around my head and upper body to hide the worst of it. Angus just has to hope for the best. With a quick mumbled request, he slides the ferryman's spare waistcoat over his torso, making himself look years older in an instant. I fidget with my skirt.

The Superintendent. He must have gone ahead of the rest of the trusty party for some reason.

No matter. If we can persuade him to abandon the plan, so much the better. There are only three others waiting by the pier, although what he is doing with these old men is beyond me. One of them even walks with a limp.

Self-conscious, I pull the shawl in around my head. Remembering the look on the man's face as the first stone landed at his feet, I fight a nervous giggle. The memory of his expensive coat, fluttering in the wind (and by then splattered with gull droppings) makes me laugh for real.

'Janet! Stop it—this is serious. You'll give us away!'

'Fine. I won't.' I take a deep breath.

'Remember our plan?'

'Yes Angus, I remember.' I don't add aloud that it was *my* plan in the first place.

The faces on the pier are drawn and I wonder what could be worrying such a man of power. Maybe he has a conscience after all.

As planned, I begin to cough as we approach, giving Angus the chance to wind the shawl even more snugly around my head. We linger while the ferryman swings over the side of the ferry and wades through the shallows to tie the knot.

'Don't tie her up, good man. We need to get across as soon as possible.' I recognise the voice of the Superintendent—so like the Schoolmaster's.

The ferryman seems undaunted. 'Gentlemen, I need to take a message to the houses yonder; then I'll be back. Make yourselves comfortable. Will you travel on or return, gentlemen?'

'Return, most certainly,' answers the Superintendent, impatience in his tone. 'You lot! On you come, let's get this over with.'

But the three men hesitate. With a glance, Angus and I decide that we have waited long enough. The time is now. We move into view and approach the plank leading to the rocky pier.

'Ah, let these young folk off first, then we'll be more comfortable,' one of the old men says.

We splash to shore. The Superintendent's eyes pass over me like a knife over soft butter, but Angus is a different matter.

'Stop a moment, lad.'

Poor Angus has no choice at all. I cough again, but the Superintendent doesn't take his eyes off him, scrutinising him from head to foot. 'How old?'

'Eighteen now,' Angus answers, and I'm awed—his voice doesn't even waver. I wipe my brow, but my acting is in vain—all four only have eyes for my brother.

'Tall enough, isn't he?' The Superintendent turns to his companions. They crowd round so closely that I can't tell who is speaking.

'Feel his arms. There's a bit of strength here all right.'

'No weapon though.'

'That can be seen to.'

Angus turns his face to the sky as they prod and discuss. I decide to have another go, coughing and leaning on the side of the boat. The Superintendent ignores me and sidles up to Angus.

'Lad, I'll pay you good money if you leave the girl behind and join us. There's a village needs teaching a lesson, and we're here to enforce the law. I'll pay you.' His voice is smooth. 'Handsomely.'

Angus moves away with a determined step and puts his arm around me. 'Gentlemen, forgive me—I promised to take my sister to safety. You can see she is sickly and I need to get her away from Rispond as soon as possible, with the big rebellion gathering. There's bound to be fighting. Excuse me—she's only twelve.'

I can't imagine why, but the three old men are exchanging glances and one by one, they back away from the boat. The Superintendent rolls his eyes.

The first man, a wizened, white-haired, weather-beaten fellow, stretches his hand across and stops us. 'Hang on, lad. A rebellion?'

'They're coming from all corners to form an uprising, Sir. Gathering at Durness from goodness knows where—

there must be hundreds by now. They are sure to challenge the Master's plan with violence—and it's not safe for her.' Again, he indicates me with a sideways nod and I look down rather than meet their eyes.

There is a pause while the Superintendent tries to think of something to say, but it's too late.

'I knew there weren't enough of us,' the second man snaps. 'When you said "trusty party" I thought we'd be meeting more on the way.'

'We were!' the Superintendent protests. 'The thing is, you see, the locals are a bit reluctant. Lazy...'

'And you haven't paid us a penny yet, Superintendent. And if there's a rebellion...'

Angus squeezes my shoulder, and I'm thinking the same. *This IS the trusty party?*

'We're going no further, Superintendent. You can keep your money. I won't fight.' The second man marches away, almost colliding with the ferryman returning from his errand. His friends follow, pursued by the Superintendent who tries curses and pleas and flattery and threats, until we can't hear him anymore.

Slowly, a smile creeps across the ferryman's toothless mouth.

'You did it, didn't ye?'

As the Superintendent disappears after the men, Angus and I climb on board again, taking care to stay hidden from view.

It's a long way back from the ferry port, even though the mare is well rested and eager to trot. For the most part, Angus and I cling to her mane in silence. No triumph; no, it doesn't feel like that.

Simply a little relief and a lot of hope.

Maybe, just maybe, we have made a difference.

CHAPTER FIFTEEN

For When the Time Comes

FATHER LOOKS GRAVE. HE'S BEEN OUT IN THE FIELDS ALL DAY, but it can't have been easy, not knowing where we were. Wee Donald says the Schoolmaster called at the house in person, asking after me, so I know there'll be another beating when I return. For a brief moment, I yearn for a position in service, like Catherine. Then I remember that being a maid means working for men like Anderson and, on top of that, she has no position anymore at all.

As there is more news, we hold another meeting before dinner, only this time out in the open: the Schoolmaster has refused to unlock the schoolhouse. He stands a little way off. Hugh's eyes twinkle as he addresses the anxious faces.

'Who would like to hazard a guess at how many men the Superintendent was able to persuade to join his trusty party?'

The Schoolmaster's expression looks as if he's eaten a barrel of raw stinging nettles, washed down with a bucket of sand.

'Just say it, Hugh!' says Father and he's right. No-one is in the mood for games.

'Three.'

A gasp of surprise from all around me, and even though I saw the men flee with my own eyes, I still worry that somehow it's not the truth.

Hugh continues: 'We have it on the word of our two young eye witnesses. And old men they were at that, two of them wounded veterans. When they heard gossip of an army of volunteers from the whole of Sutherland, ready and waiting for them, prepared to fight to the death—they turned on their heels and fled. And who'd blame them?'

Hugh's eyes flit from Angus to me. He is properly chuckling now, which sounds eerie into our stunned silence. 'Well done, Angus and Janet!'

Gradually, whispers break out, then chatter, punctuated by laughter.

'Wait, Hugh. Does that mean…?' Mr Mackay from the Top House begins.

'Exactly! No trusty party is coming anymore.'

There are the beginnings of cheers, but the Reverend

rises and slowly, silence returns.

'Brothers and sisters; I think the time has come to write to the Duke of Sutherland on your behalf. Even though he may not be able to sway Anderson, he is a man of considerable influence.'

His tone changes as he proceeds. 'However, it would sadden me if the success of our cause was rooted in a lie.'

My ever-present inner guilt wields its knife again, but Hugh simply shrugs.

'This won't be the end of it. Who says it *has* to be a lie? Let's make it true and raise an army. For when the time comes.' He looks directly at the Reverend. 'For—mark my words —it will surely come.'

Later that night, my lids droop as I cook the first bere scone on the griddle while the cabbage soup boils in the pot above.

'Janet,' Granna's voice accuses as she scrapes the burnt mess off the griddle. 'Wherever is your head tonight? We still need to eat, so I'll thank you for not throwing good grain into the fire!' She slaps me over the back of the head, but gently.

'Sorry,' I mumble and add the next dollop of mixture, coughing until the burnt smoke has found an escape through the thatch. My eyes water and I turn away from the fire to watch her. *How lined Granna's face is, as if the glimmer of the fire carves out new cracks in her skin.*

'What are you looking at?' She stops hanging the washing and stares. 'Janet, the scone…'

I spin round and get to it just in time.

'I'd better sit with you, girl. You've been very headstrong today. Very headstrong.'

I nod and allow my body to sag sideways into her slight frame with all my weight. *So tired, so, so tired…*

My head sinks onto her shoulder and the last thing I remember is the scent of soup and fresh scone and leaning into my Granna's love.

I think she must have put a blanket over me after I slid to the floor. Was it Angus or Father who lifted me into the good box bed, I wonder? I wake in the early hours of the night, wrapped in a shawl and a blanket with wind and rain battling against the house.

Grey sky presses down on me the next morning, but Mother will not yield.

'You'll be late and you'll only have yourself to blame. You may have done a good thing yesterday, but today you go to school, and that is all there is to it.'

I clutch my stomach, but to no avail. I rub my head, even

retch a couple of times, but she remains unmoved. When I try limping, she finally loses patience. 'For goodness' sake Janet, no wonder the Schoolmaster is at his wit's end with you. I have a mind to agree with him!' I can't help laughing then and she gives me a playful skelp with her cloth.

At school, I bear the beating with as much dignity as I can muster.

Not a waking moment passes without my thinking of the trusty party. Who will the wicked Superintendent bring next?

Armed ruffians? Soldiers bearing weapons, ready to attack our own?

Hugh.

Father.

Even Angus?

Only Mary's lads even remotely look like fighters. Surely Mr Top House Mackay would struggle to fit his considerable bulk into any kind of uniform? I sigh and pull the cat onto my lap; a little comfort; a little warmth. Until I think of another cat all those years ago. The one Granna told me about.

Strathnaver 1814: The Cat

The evil in the air was palpable. Noise of hoof beats, shouting and goading, and soul-damning curses from the mouths of the thugs, swigging whisky and spreading flames and death. Anna could barely breathe. 'No John, please! They have weapons.'

But her husband didn't listen. 'Master Sellar, the woman in yonder house is old and ill. Have mercy. Allow us to make arrangements and...'

The hard thud of wood on skull hurt Anna as if she herself had been struck. Like a scarecrow, her husband crumpled to the ground. Another magnified thud as his jaw hit the rocks. Anna lurched forward. The Factor was urging his men on from a distance, but their laughter and shouts meant nothing now.

'John! JOHN!'

It took all her strength to drag his limp body the short distance to the rock face where Anna had wrapped Wee Johnnie in curtain fabric to sleep. Her husband was breathing —thank the Lord.

Anna dropped to her knees to pray while she pressed a cold wet cloth to his temple where Sellar's baton had hit. Old Maggie from next door hobbled towards them and sank to the ground, weeping silently.

Anna barely noticed the orange and gold reflection of their flaming roof on her husband's face, but then a new noise startled her. A high-pitched screech. Who was trapped? A quick glance at the hillside, but no, all the neighbours were accounted for. It was coming from her own house, now hidden in flame and smoke.

The answer shot out between the legs of one of the thugs who was trying, but failing, to push in the side wall. Anna felt a rush of pride. Her husband was a good builder.

The black cat slowed as soon as it got to the open air.

'Throw it back in! Let's see what it does!'

Anna couldn't see the speaker—a hoarse voice on the other side of the house. But she did see the ruffian reach down, pick up the helpless animal and throw it through the window, back into the burning house.

'No!' Anna flew at the man who stood with bent knees and outstretched arms, ready to stop the pet. But two more men had dismounted now, taking swigs from a bottle. She felt herself pulled off and thrown against the rocks where she slid to the ground.

'There it is!' The cat was caught in mid-jump as it shot out through the burning doorway.

'Again! I'll bar the entrance,' the man rasped.

'Are you human at all? May the Lord punish you for what you have done! May he...'

But Anna's voice finally gave way, all her pain and fear and outrage silenced.

The cat was hurled through the blazing window for the last time, and the men mounted their horses and trotted further up the valley, not even looking over their shoulders.

Crackling flames drowned the animal's final squeals as smoke consumed the last of the roof.

Anna sank back, pulling the sleeping toddler to herself for comfort.

Chapter Sixteen

Preparations

The Reverend stays at Hugh's house late into the night to compose the message to the surrounding villages.

The next morning Hector, Angus, Peggy and I are tasked with taking it to the nearby townships, while Mary's lads will ride the mare and travel as far as Oldshoremore down the coast.

The boys are sent east and Peggy and I head west towards Durine.

After walking side by side in silence for a mile, I try. 'Peggy, it'll be a long day if you refuse to speak to me at all.'

Stubbornly, she turns her head to the hills and lifts her dress so it doesn't catch the mud.

I sigh. 'Fine. Be like that. But you're wasting your time there. I think you can't help getting it at least a little bit dirty.'

She snorts and lifts it higher just to spite me. I steal a sideways look. Even under her lined hood, I can see the pile of braids, so carefully pinned into place, while half my loose bun blows in the wind already. I tuck most of it under my plain woven shawl.

'I think it'll rain soon,' I begin again. It doesn't look like she is going to answer that one either. We walk on half a mile and I begin to wonder if I could bring myself to apologise to her for what happened at the burn.

'I don't care what you think, Janet.'

'Yes! You spoke! Peggy, aren't your arms sore, gathering your dress like that?'

'I don't want to look like a savage or a highwayman when we deliver the messages. And, Janet, I think you should let *me* speak when we get there. The more civilised we behave the...'

She is too busy lecturing me to notice the muddy puddle; stepping in, sliding out and landing in it on her back. It takes all my self-control not to dissolve into fits of laughter, but the Reverend did say "*as far as it depends on you, be at peace with one another*". So far I haven't done very well.

'Quick, Peggy, take my hand before it soaks in!'

I haul her up and inspect the damage. She is still gasping with the cold. I drag the soaking coat off her and throw my own around her shoulders, rubbing her back. And she lets me. Silent tears run down her cheeks and she keeps looking down at her stained dress.

'Don't worry. *I'll* try to sound civilised, and you can take the blanket from the bundle and wrap it round yourself. Look; it's not far now.'

The skies choose this very moment to release a flood of rain, and by the time we deliver our first message in Smoo, both of us look as if Highwaymen had tried to drown us in a bog. We push on to Sangomore, finishing with Durine and Balnakeil in the late afternoon. All the way back, we cling to one another for warmth, tugging at the blanket and even giggling between our sneezes.

'Good Lord, Janet; off with these clothes! And be quick about it!' Granna loses no time, pulling and pushing at me until I obey. My nose drips and I shiver, but the hot brew and a seat by the hearth go a long way to improve my mood.

By the time Angus returns from the inland settlements, I'm snoozing. The mare's clip-clopping wakes me up once more when the moon is already high in the sky. Mary's boys are back.

The next morning, messengers start arriving at Ceannabeinne from all over. Father is summoned to Hugh's house. The Reverend is already there, and the steady stream of visitors ebbs and flows. Some of this I see and some of it I hear: an unfamiliar step, a strange voice...

Of course, I *should* be at the schoolhouse, *not* poking my nose into affairs that I may not understand—at least that's what Granna thinks. But Mother takes one look at me and stands stock-still.

'Heavens, Janet, look at you!'

I'm puzzled, because I can't look at me without a looking glass, and looking glasses are in short supply here. That would be different if I lived in the Top House, of course.

'Janet! Didn't you hear?' Mother sounds distant somehow, even though she is standing right in front of me. 'I said get into the bed right now, lass. You're swaying. Here, Anna, help me with Janet a moment, please.'

Granna emerges from the steam of the pot and hooks her arm under mine while Mother takes the other. 'There!'

I sink onto the good bed, normally reserved for Mother and Father, but I'm too weak to ask questions. In any case, my legs have turned to sludge and the mattress catches my dead weight.

Mother reaches for the bedding. 'You might have caught your death in that rain. And Angus and Hector, too. I wonder if Peggy is as bad.'

Involuntarily, she turns her head in the direction of the Top House, even though she won't see anything through the wall, with the window being so tiny.

119

'Peggy will be worse than me. She fell in the puddle,' I say, but somehow it all comes out wrong.

Mother scrutinises me for a second. 'Anna, she's feverish. She's trying to speak, but it's all gibberish. What shall we do?'

'Pack the blankets on top of her and hope she sweats it out. Nothing else for it.'

I'm shivering, even though one, two and three blankets are stretched over me, one after the other. *Am I going to suffocate?* Mother tucks two more blankets tightly around my face and feet, so that the heaviness itself lulls me to sleep. The last thing I notice is that my throat is on fire, which is odd because throats don't really go on fire.

Do they?

Strathnaver 1814: The Chill of Rocks and Hearts

The smouldering piles of stones glowed against the gathering dark, hissing as stray raindrops fell.

'All of them?' Anna repeated.

'Yes,' John answered, sinking onto the rocks beside his wife and rubbing the bump on his aching head. 'I walked all the way to Hope and it's the same. All the walls pushed in. Nothing but rubble.'

Anna said nothing. While the men were away, she had seen to the little one and tried to hold old Maggie's hand, but the aged woman was barely stirring now. Maggie's son in law, Chisholm, had gone to fetch help.

'It'll be raining hard soon. We'll need to get her comfortable and sheltered.'

Together, Anna and John lifted Old Maggie into their own box bed and draped over the curtain fabric which had covered the doorway of their longhouse—when their longhouse still stood.

It was hard to remember it there, only this morning, where the smoking stones now lay scattered.

Anna pulled the blanket tight around her neighbour's wrinkled face, saying a silent prayer. 'There you are, Maggie. We can't make you comfortable, but this is the best we can do.'

The rain fell freely as John and Anna huddled together to shelter Wee Johnnie from the worst of the wind.

Chapter Seventeen

Truce

THE COLD SPOON TOUCHES MY LIPS AND I OPEN THEM, unsure whether it's a dream. It's so cool, so smooth. I want it to stay on my lips forever...

Until the strong nettle brew trickles down my throat and I splutter upright and retch.

'Janet! Stay still girl, or else it'll spill!'

There's an idea.

Mother pushes me back down and I force my eyes open, but too late. The spoon is coming towards me again at lightning speed, and now I have no choice but to *see* the dark green slimy liquid. I open my mouth to protest, but this is all the opportunity my mother needs. 'Ha-ha! There you have it. It's not that hard!'

My face pulls into a grimace—I haven't the energy to resist.

'And another one.' It sounds like a threat, but she's

already fulfilled it. I want to sit upright, heave, wriggle; but the heavy blankets mean that my face is the only part of me with any room for manoeuvre. Resigned, I open my mouth properly and my mother tips what feels like a bucketful down my throat.

I'm going to die. Surely I am.

And my eyes close until darkness and silence surround me once more.

I wake in the dead of night, soundless apart from the wind, the thrashing surf and Father's snoring. How long have I been sleeping?

No-one can tell me the answer to that question, but Angus, too, is shaken by a cough, wheezing while he turns; the straw in the mattress crinkling with every move.

My hair hangs wet across my forehead and sticks to my crusty eyelids. I rub my eyes and stare at the roof thatch— or I *would* if it was not invisible in the blanket of darkness that would suffocate me if I let it.

Then it starts.

My body behaves as if it didn't belong to me. Apart from being on fire, and wet with sweat, I have now lost all control over my movement. My feet start dancing and an echoing drum bangs inside my head with an unbearable beat. My hands twitch in time with the pain while the darkness continues to gag me to the point of sickness. Then a girl's scream cuts through the smoky air.

'Bring the light, quick, Angus. Hurry!' It's Mother.

'What's happening? What's happening to her? Why is she screaming like that?' Angus's voice sounds so much higher than it really is, as if he is years younger.

'It's the fever, son. Have you got the water? Could you wipe her brow? I'll go to fetch help. Father's still at Hugh's. Good, Angus; see if she'll take a drink.' Mother sounds frantic, as if someone is in danger. I feel cold metal against my mouth again and I want to shriek for more. *Empty the bucket over me*, I want to yell, *put the fire out! Can't you see that I'm burning?*

But like the rest of my body, my mouth won't obey me anymore.

And then I'm sinking, thrashing to keep the fiery floods at bay. Again and again, strong hands pin me down. *Don't they know I am drowning in flames*? Voices speak soothingly. *Can't they feel the prongs of pain, piercing the last of my strength?*

There is a light, somewhere above, but my eyelids refuse to open. I feel a weight over my chest, as if someone was leaning over, and a deep calm voice says something, but I forget what it is before he's even finished speaking. The voice is familiar. Or is it?

And then all voices mix together with the drum of pain in my head, louder and louder, faster and faster. Invisible forces seem to pull my limbs left and right.

Until the light goes out and there is only silence.

I wake from my sleep, but the pain is still there. It's like ten thousand Schoolmasters have spent ten thousand years beating me with ten thousand tawses, and I'm still not sure that covers it. Granna sits by my bed in the dull light of day, slouched over in a kind of semi-nap. Angus and Father are nowhere to be seen.

My mouth feels as if it's full of stones, but it's worth a try. 'Granna…'

It doesn't even sound like the word, but it's enough. She bounces upright and leans close to my face.

'Janet, lass. Oh, Janet!'

And hot salty drops land on my cheek and are vigorously stroked away. Granna's hair is still in a plait: she's not even got dressed properly, and when she runs to the door, her nightgown blows in the wind beneath the shawl.

'Janet's woken up! JANET'S WOKEN UP!'

The slashing pain in my head returns at her volume, but it seems to have the desired effect—footsteps on the path, subtle thuds, but urgent. Mother, Father, Angus and Granna bustle in. I move slowly, like under water, but I manage to hold my head up and open my eyes, making a careful attempt at a smile.

And Father, of all people, hurls himself down on my bed, burying his face in the blankets.

There is a long pause before he speaks, and, like the man Father is, it's short, and to the point.

'We thought we'd lost you, lass...'

At least two days—I can't be sure—pass in a haze of sleep and sweat, but eventually, I venture out of the box bed, steadying myself against the wooden bedstead and look out. It's almost as if summer had decided that enough was enough. The sunshine still beats down from above, but the wind is sharp now. Not long till the autumn solstice, and still no word from Dornoch. Would the Superintendent give up and leave us be? Not likely.

'What day is it, Granna?'

'Saturday. Almost a week since you fell ill, lass.'

For the first time since we stumbled along the rain-sodden path together, I think of Peggy Mackay.

'Mother, did Peggy ever get ill that day, too? She was wetter than me; so bad that I let her have my shawl.'

Mother and Granna exchange a look.

'What?' I sway slightly and lean against the dresser to regain my balance. 'What is it?'

'Rest a while longer, lass and leave the worrying to others,' Granna answers in her sing-song voice and a knot forms in my stomach.

'No, I will not rest a while longer! Not until you tell me. About Peggy.'

With renewed resolve, I haul myself upright by the bedpost and stagger over to Granna where she crouches by the hearth. I nearly stumble into the fire, but Mother's strong arms guide me sideways.

'There, Janet, wrap this around yourself to keep warm. And, to answer your question, yes, Peggy did get very ill. Very ill indeed.'

'But now she's fine. She is, isn't she? Isn't she, Granna?'

The hesitation is all the confirmation I need. Still unsteady on my feet, I wobble through the door, through the garden, past the dyke and the burn and upwards, upwards, upwards.

To the Top House.

By the time I reach the door, I feel like the hills are spinning with the clouds, but I need to see Peggy. Mother and Granna shout for me to come back, and soon I feel

Mother's gentle pressure on my arm, trying to ease me away, downhill, back to the house. But no; there is a limit to what a conscience can bear, and this is the limit of mine. I *wanted* to see her fall; I emptied the dirty water over her at the well and I made fun of her. What I want *now* is very simple.

Peggy Mackay must not die.

I elbow Mother away and renew my knocking, stronger this time.

Finally, I hear steps inside. Of course, Mr Mackay and Hector must be away, doing man-like things like fishing or hunting. *Providing*—now that Anderson doesn't keep any of us in his pay. The steps drag slowly along the flagstone floor, echoing slightly. The door creaks open and Mrs Mackay stands before us.

At least I *think* it is Mrs Mackay. Her hair hangs loose down her shoulders with her blouse untucked and her back-to-front skirt stained, eyes bloodshot like a soldier.

If Mother is as shocked as I am, she hides it well.

'I am sorry to disturb you at a time like this. Janet simply wouldn't be persuaded to stay away.'

I can barely croak: 'Let me see Peggy. Please, please Mrs Mackay, let me see her!'

Without waiting, I push past the woman and walk right into the Top House. I don't need directions either. The fire burns brightly on the gable hearth and Peggy's whimpering fills me with a relief the ocean would struggle to hold.

'She's not woken yet. Only this. Like an animal: twitching, moaning.' Mrs Mackay's voice sounds dead and Mother embraces her in a swift movement which surprises me. But Mrs Mackay yields, burying her head in Mother's hair and sobbing soundlessly.

I approach the jerking bundle of blanket that I know is Peggy. Sitting by the end, I begin to talk, leaning over her and whispering so that only she can hear.

'So Peggy. We both caught a fever in all that rain. I know how you feel—I was the same until yesterday. And listen: I'm sorry for being unkind to you; I truly am. I think that, maybe just for now, we should call a truce? What do you think?' And then I bow my head and pray, silently, for the good Lord to heal and restore and all the other fancy bible words the Reverend uses. The whimpering eases and behind me, Mother's soothing words to Mrs Mackay mingle with my mumbled pleas.

Peggy's legs relax. Her hands twitch across her body one

last time and she lies still.

The silence is worse than what went before.

Much, much worse.

I look at Mother, alarmed. Mrs Mackay rushes to clutch Peggy's hand.

Then Peggy's body convulses in a deep, gasping breath.

And she opens her eyes.

CHAPTER EIGHTEEN

The Procession

MY BALANCE DESERTS ME AND I SINK ONTO THE SMOOTH flagstone floor, leaning against the whitewashed wall. This house is so much lighter than ours, so much warmer too. The sunshine adds a heavenly glow: the answer to my prayers. Peggy doesn't speak, not yet—but she is breathing and nods in response to her mother's words.

'Come on, lass… Janet, come on,' Mother urges quietly in my ear. 'Give Peggy a chance to rest now the worst is over.' She gestures down and I realise I'm still only wearing a nightgown and a shawl, stained from treading on it on the way up the path.

'Let's get you dressed, and then you'll need to…'

Raised voices distract both of us, and even Mrs Mackay looks up briefly. She bends her head to tend Peggy again.

I can hear Granna over the din. The words are muffled, but the mood beneath them travels right through the walls and windows—and chills the core of my heart. One glance at Mother, and both of us rush through the door and into the open to see.

The villagers all watch, from their houses and byres, from the fields and from the hill. Two lone figures look up from the beach; probably Father and Angus. All of us stand, like statues, because, rounding the Rispond bend is a procession. I draw the shawl closer around my shoulders and wait. Passing the schoolhouse, they come into view. They don't turn down into our village though, just keep riding towards Durine.

There are how many... ten, twelve, fourteen special constables? I've seen pictures of their uniform at the schoolhouse, but never for real. Mother's arm pulls me tighter. Two gentlemen ride with the constables, and with a pang of guilt and anger, I recognise the Superintendent of Dornoch. He glances down the hill to see his own Mackintosh coat flutter above the burn on the pole, but then stares straight ahead.

The other gentleman is dressed even more ornately. The whiteness of his ruffled collar is almost blinding, with a shining metal star and the Sutherland coat of arms pinned to a ceremonial robe no doubt intended to impress his importance on us all.

No stones.

No shouts.

We're all out of ideas.

Strathnaver, 1814: Another Procession

A procession of a different kind wound its way towards the sea. Few horses, no torches, just a tired trickle of people carrying what was left of their lives from the mountains to the sea. Ben Hope spiked the sky like a hopeless prayer.

'The church, too? They burned the church?' Anna asked, shaking her head as if, somehow, this could make it not true.

John nodded, feeling the lump on the side of his head. He had barely spoken since two days hence. At least the owner of the Rispond estate had agreed to take some of them in. The land was bad over that way. What could you grow in a place where rocks rub against sand and the sea winds batter the shore?

'We'll make do.'

Anna tightened the cloth that held Wee Johnnie to her back and turned to check on Maggie in the cart again.

'So, her son-in-law is on his way?'

John nodded. 'By the sounds of it, he is a tinker. We'll need to take her with us until he gets here—and let's hope he does.'

133

Making camp beside other families near the shore, John counted what was left of their money again. 'I'm not sure it'll be enough for the ferry, but we'll have to try. We need to get her to shelter.'

'Yes.'

John sighed, tucking the money back into his shirt and wrapped the two woollen blankets around Anna and the child. Buttoning his coat up to the top, he curled up beside the fire.

Neither of them was surprised at what they found the next morning.

Old Maggie was dead.

*

Once the endless line of special constables has passed us by, movement spreads like flames on dry heath. Father and Angus clamber up from the beach. Before long, a huddle of worry has formed around Hugh, but for once, even he looks like he simply doesn't know what to do.

His indecision doesn't last long.

'Hector, Angus—I have no doubt that Anderson has brought this visit upon us. Go after them and find out where they are staying. I will see the Reverend and decide what's best to do. Bring me news there as soon as you have it.'

The boys jog up to the road, following the procession at a safe distance. Hugh, meanwhile, steps back and addresses the village at large.

'Pray,' is all he says, before striding back to his hut to fetch his coat. Granna sinks onto her knees right there, alongside Margaret Munro, and their pleas pierce the air in the darkening sky. Mary's boys saddle the two horses and disappear along the road. Hector and Angus must have gone on elsewhere, for neither of them reappear even as darkness gathers. Granna and Mother see to the fire, but no-one thinks to prepare food. Father went with Hugh, so no-one knows when he'll be back.

Dressed and upright, I almost wish I was still feverish so I couldn't ask myself questions. Imagination is a terrible thing.

I shudder to think what the gleaming swords and pistols of the special constables could do to my peace-loving father, my headstrong brother, my elderly village leader...

It's no good; I need to get out.

'I'll get water for the cattle,' I offer.

'No, Janet, you're still pale. It's better if we wait until you are well.'

'But Mother, what if Angus and Father don't come back? In time,' I add when Granna's face falls. 'I'll do it. Please.'

I would like to pray for their safety, but Peggy woke. My heart simply doesn't have the faith to ask the good Lord for more.

I glance at the clouds above me while I stumble to the spring in the twilight. Dark and light, swirling together in ever-changing patterns. Red for blood, black for evil, gold for God.

And a thousand shades in between.

What will become of us?

A noise on the path startles me so much that I drop the pail. In turn, a hooded figure hurrying up to the road exclaims in fear. Wait! That sounded like...

I step forward. 'Is that you Catherine? What are you doing out at this time of night?'

'And m-me.' Wee Donald steps out from under her coat, wrapped up so thickly I thought he was an animal at first.

'Where are you two going?'

'To Durine. Father and Mother both went there. It's where the constables and the gentlemen are staying. The Durine Inn.'

I step closer so I can see her face properly. Catherine's voice is determined.

'Janet, I know what the Master Anderson is capable of. But our father thinks there is still hope, and most of the men have gone to plead our case. Even our mother went with him. She says she couldn't bear to lose a husband and she'd rather die with him. And maybe she thinks that the constables will be more lenient with a woman present. They told me to watch Donald and guard the fire, but, oh Janet…'

Her face twists in anguish and Wee Donald sums it up as it is.

'Catherine's w-worried and she can't s-sit still and she put the fire right out. And we're g-going to Durine now. To h-help.'

I hesitate. But only for a second.

'Give me a minute,' I breathe, thinking fast. 'Because I'm coming with you.'

Creeping into the byre, with my pail splashing as I shake, I take a woollen saddle blanket for warmth. Praying for forgiveness, I close the byre gate as slowly and quietly as I ever have, and speed through the darkness after my friends.

The moon has risen a little above the horizon, casting ghostly shadows onto the road as we run. Even from Smoo, we can see torches, flickering menacingly in the night. When we reach Sangomore, the countless angry voices of the mob carry on the wind, and we almost run the final stretch to Durine.

CHAPTER NINETEEN

Torches at the Inn

'Do you think we should stay back? Just in case we're seen?' Catherine sounds uncertain and Wee Donald looks to me.

I squint to see. 'Maybe. Is that Hugh over there? By the gate?'

'Think s-so.'

It's hard to make out faces through the crowd, but Catherine is probably right—we should avoid being seen. I guide Wee Donald towards a small stone dyke and push aside some branches of the scrub beneath. The ground slopes slightly, affording us a better view of the crowd than closer up. Huddling together for warmth, each of us is left to our own thoughts. I busy myself counting: the crowd here goes far beyond Ceannabeinne men, or even women. First, I account for Father, then all other men from the village. All there, most of them standing near Hugh. Wait, no, the

Schoolmaster isn't here, but that doesn't surprise me much.

'Catherine,' I whisper. 'Do you recognise any of these other people?'

'Some, but not many. Some are from over the other side of Rispond. Who is in charge, do you think?'

It's as if the torch-bearing mob had heard our confusion, for at that moment Hugh's familiar call rings out across the crowd. For a moment, I wonder if the important officials only speak English. Surely they must be scared inside the inn; listening but not understanding?

The door of the inn has opened and the Reverend Findlater emerges, his face grave. Behind him, the innkeeper seems to be making placating gestures. When he is ignored, he retreats into the building, slamming the wooden door behind him.

'Friends! Peace! Listen to the Reverend Findlater.' Hugh shouts, and I realise: I have never actually heard him shout before. His authority is instant and absolute. The torches illuminate his face as he nods to the Reverend who addresses the crowd.

'Brothers and sisters. In this inn behind me, I pleaded with a Mr Fraser, none less than the Procurator Fiscal of Sutherland himself. He and the Sheriff Superintendent who is known to some of you, remain unmoved.' He raises his eyes to the heavens. 'The townships must be cleared, as the law demands.'

The Reverend drops his head, and someone from the crowd takes his chance.

'But what about the harvest? And none of us have anywhere to go!' asks Kenneth, Mary's younger boy.

Someone else interjects even as the crowd roar their agreement. New people arrive all the time. We must be approaching a hundred now. A Balnakeil man speaks up.

'Yes! And if the Rispond Estate is cleared, all the Duke's lands are bound to follow. I'm not being forced out of my home yet, but I'll be no man if I allow this injustice to go unchallenged. We're bound to be next.'

I don't know the bearded man, but again, a sizeable wave of support crashes through the crowd. The Reverend raises his hand, and silence once more descends, like a lid onto a boiling pot.

'There's more,' Findlater continues.

A pause.

Why doesn't he speak?

Tell us!

He looks like he is fighting a battle with himself until honesty gains the upper hand.

'Force may be used against you, if you resist,' the

Reverend goes on, and I shiver. 'You will be evicted... '

But nothing prepares me for what he says next.

'Tomorrow. On the Sabbath.'

And these are the last words I hear before the pot boils over, exploding its pent-up anger and aggression all over Durine.

Without meaning to, I claw my fingernails into Wee Donald's hand: the crowd surges towards the inn with a roar. Donald yelps and I relax my grip, distracted by what I see: men lurching forward, banging on the door of the inn, climbing over the stone wall to get nearer, reaching for the windows.

And he's gone.

'Donald! Come back!' Catherine jumps up, too. The shadowy outline of her brother gets smaller, running and blurring in the torchlight.

'DONALD!'

But he can't hear us at all. I understand: all *he* can see is his frightened-looking mother in the midst of all this fiery fury.

With a desperate glance at one another, Catherine and I pelt after him. Before long, I can't see Wee Donald or Catherine anymore; they are swallowed, like me, by the pulsing mass of bodies. Somehow, I find myself at the front. My ears are so full of noise that, actually, I'm not hearing anything at all anymore. I see the Reverend raise his hands to gain control of the crowd.

To no avail.

He raises his hands again, but this time to pray. His eyes close; and right there, at the core of the chaos, he offers his silent pleas to God.

There is banging on the door, but the innkeeper would be mad to answer it. Then it happens; an ear-splitting, splintering noise. It is followed by more and more of the same: new feet kicking against the inn door. When it finally gives way, there's a cheer from the crowd, and without knowing why, I join in. The odd thing is, no-one seems to want to be first to enter. It's as if the whole crowd holds its breath.

A low voice. 'HALT! Listen! In the name of all that's decent and holy, STAY BACK!' It's Hugh.

What follows isn't silence; there's too much anger for that, and our elder can barely make himself heard.

'Friends, your anger is righteous and it would take hold of my heart, too. But I fear that bloodshed will only do more harm.'

There is a rumble of angry muttering. Bloodshed is *very* much on some people's minds—there's no doubting that. I pull the saddle blanket around my ears—the last thing I want is for Father or Angus to recognise me.

'Bloodshed will only lead to more bloodshed; take it from an old man who knows. Evicting us on the Sabbath, however, is an affront to all Christian decency. A delegation of us will go into the inn and speak—again—with the gentlemen. Until then—can I trust you all to hold your peace?'

Voices around me mutter, but Hugh barely pauses for a second before bellowing: 'CAN I?'

Several men and women shout 'Aye.' Others yell 'Don't be long' and 'Stand your ground, though.' I'm close enough to see Hugh nod to Father, Mr Mackay from the Top House and a couple of other men I don't know, although I've seen their faces before. The Reverend pushes aside the parts of the splintered door which still bar the way and steps in ahead of the group.

I feel a small, sweaty hand wriggle its way into mine.

'Donald.'

'This way, J-Janet!' He pulls me sideways and back towards a small group of women. Catherine and her parents are already there.

And Mother.

My heart tilts when I see the expression on her face.

Waiting is hard. The moon glides on regardless, high in the sky, when the Reverend and our men return to the crowd. A few roadside fires, kindled with driftwood and peat, warm the small groups huddled beside them. A Durine woman has brought two pots of broth which we share as best as we can, giving the ladle a wipe before passing it on to the person beside.

Mother has not spoken since she scolded me in front of the world. As dread floods my mind, her words are the flotsam and jetsam in it: *Only just recovered... Your grandmother has had enough suffering without worrying about you again and again... too headstrong... you think you're an adult, but... proud... conceited... do as you please without a thought for those who care for you... disobedient... always in trouble at school... no wonder...*

And what does it matter? I know she is simply voicing her worry and fear. I know it, but still I struggle to be meek; to submit and ask forgiveness.

Maybe she is even right.

And tomorrow. The Sabbath. The holy day of God.

Will we sit on the hillside with a wobbly cairn of goods? All

we own in the world, piled high, like Granna before?
The sky the only roof over our heads?
Watching our home burn for sheep?

All of us rise to our feet, waiting for the Reverend to speak, but he nods to Hugh.

His voice sounds dry and cracked.

'They won't listen. Even Monday is too late for them. They won't listen.'

The uproar which follows shakes the earth as it splits the skies.

CHAPTER TWENTY

A Force for Good

THINGS HAPPEN FAST AFTER THAT, SO VERY FAST. New torches are kindled in the roadside fires. A mob of our men kicks what is left of the door out of the way and so many *try* to enter the inn all at once that, at the start, no-one gets through. But one after the other, they thunder into the inn. The innkeeper's voice is heard, but I can't make out what he's saying, only the pleading tone which stops abruptly. There are clashes inside, metal on metal. I strain and struggle against Mother who has clamped her arm around me from behind, unyielding.

'Let me go, Mother! Angus...'

Yes, my brother is in there. I saw him squeeze through the splintered doorway, straight after Mary's boys and young MacIntosh, followed by I-don't-know who. But the special constables in that inn are soldiers—armed, skilled, hardened...

Mother must read my mind.

'You're *not* going in there, Janet. That's exactly why I wanted you to stay home—because this is the sort of thing you'd do.' Her grip tightens and I sink into her—not to cry but to avert my eyes. Smoke is rising from the inn now and the innkeeper and his wife have emerged, running for pails of water and cursing the Superintendent and the Procurator Fiscal loudly to anyone who would listen.

'L-look, Janet!' Wee Donald and Catherine are beside us again and I follow where Donald is pointing.

Catherine screws up her eyes to see. 'Is that…?'

'Looks like it. A special constable. Don't you think?'

A fleeing figure disappears into the darkness.

There is a scream. A woman from Sangomore hobbles in our direction and Mother finally lets go of me. As the woman draws near, I see a trickle of blood down the side of her head, glistening in the moonlight.

Catherine and Wee Donald have moved forward, too. Another constable climbs out of the window. Desperately, the innkeeper's wife runs to the spring with her pail again.

Catherine and I exchange a glance. 'Come on,' I shout, for the noise is near deafening now. Every house has an outbuilding and every outbuilding is full of old pots, pails and tools. Durine is no exception. Wee Donald is glad of

147

something to do, too, filling and filling ever-new vessels by the spring while Catherine and I run to and fro, passing the water to the grateful innkeeper. Hugh catches my eye once. A shadow of surprise crosses his face, but then he nods. 'Be a force for good, Janet!' he shouts as we pass. 'It's all I can tell you in these times.'

Father directs the walking wounded to the roadside fire where Mother tends them and the Reverend comforts them. I'm out of breath, but at least I'm helping someone, and when things are as they are today, I'll settle for that very gladly. The smoke from the inn is hardly noticeable now and I allow myself a few seconds—there is a galloping sound. Who is joining us now, when things have already come to a head?

No-one at all. In fact, somehow, the two high and mighty gentlemen from Dornoch have got hold of their horses and are digging their spurs in. One of the animals rears and the crowd shrink back, giving the riders just enough room to charge through the pool of torchlight. All our men and women whip insults after them and the officials spit back with at least as much venom. How devilish and alien the English tongue sounds right now.

'W-watch, Janet!' Wee Donald screams. Some men with pitchforks have barred the Procurator Fiscal's way. He jerks the reins around and is urging his horse into a fast gallop —right at me, standing in the dark with my empty pail.

I feel myself lose balance as Wee Donald crashes into me with all the power such a small and skinny body can muster. Both of us end up in a heap on the ground and the horse's heavy hoofs pulverise the bracken right beside my head.

It takes a while for me to be able to breathe again. By then, the hoof-beats are so distant on the road that it's hard to imagine they were ever a threat at all. Catherine helps both of us up and points out the rest of the soldiers, fleeing after their masters. Into fields, hiding behind corn stooks or heading into the hills; anything *but* facing this mob of us who ask only one thing.

To have a roof over our heads tomorrow night.

We manage to count off all but one of the officers, but Wee Donald thinks he was the one who ran first.

As soon as I have my breath back, I look for my parents. I was expecting another row from Mother, but she wastes no time on that. In fact, she barely looks up from bandaging a young man's head with her shawl.

'Janet, your Grandmother is on her own. Angus is a faster runner, but…'

She doesn't need to explain the 'but'. Angus is lying on

149

the ground beside the roadside fire, holding a rolled up apron over a deep slash on his leg. His breeches are blood-soaked, but somehow she has managed to stem the flow. Father kneels beside, holding the injured leg up high on his shoulder to help with the blood loss.

'And with all these officers out there somewhere...' Mother trails off.

'Janet.' And again, this is all my Father has to say. The one word, saturated in his thanks and his love.

Mother is right. What's to stop these officers rushing to Ceannabeinne right now? Torching roofs? Burning, killing...

And Granna all on her own...

Oh Granna...

'And bring the mare, Janet, when you return. I fear Angus won't walk for a while.'

Mother is at her best when things look worst. I embrace her, place a kiss on Angus's and Father's forehead and dash into the darkness.

Considering how many people are still outside the inn in Durine, it's remarkable that no more are on the road. I run, thinking of Granna as I leave the bright, flickering glow of Durine, past Sangomore and towards Smoo, watching my step carefully with the cliffs and the cave beneath. Clouds are on the march and threaten to take away what little moonlight there is.

Come to think of it, I've never been out on my own this late. Never when it's been this dark.

My heart skips a beat as an owl glides over me and on to the machair below the road. Every rustle and shriek of the night, normally nothing but a muffled backdrop for stories by the fireside, is now magnified by fear: menacing and murderous. I strain my ears to hear the hoof beats of the Procurator Fiscal's mount, but he must be gone. The rolling in of the distant breakers is like the comforting presence of a friend. The sea is here. I may be in the dark, but I'm not alone.

We're *all* in the dark about our future.

Immediately, I feel the guilt. It should be easy for me, I suppose, with a life to live, healthy and strong—if you don't count the last few days, that is. What about the infirm, the old? What about Isabella? Hugh and Margaret? Even Granna? What will they do? The village would see to them in their hour of need.

But what if there is no village?

Determination builds again in my heart. A force for good.

It comforts me, thinking of someone in Ceannabeinne, chanting a name with every running step—and when I run out of names I do it all over again.

Rounding the corner after Smoo, I breathe deeply once more. If our village was burning, I'd see from here. I stop and bend over my knees to breathe and immediately wish I hadn't.

Because, behind me, there are heavy footsteps on the road.

I furrow my forehead and narrow my eyes but, apart from a distant glow over Durine way, the darkness hides all but shadows. The steps approach rapidly and I glance around me.

Where? Where can I hide? Good Lord, I must be quick!

For the first time in hours, I remember how sick I've been. Panic collides with nausea in my stomach and the impact nearly knocks me off my feet. *It's too late to hide.*

I sink to the ground at the side of the road where the darkness is densest.

The heavy steps round the corner…

And I hold my breath and crouch low by the rocks.

Chapter Twenty-One

The Road

THE FOOTSTEPS COME TO A HALT AND I CAN HEAR THE HOARSE breath of a man. The more I stare, the more a fuzzy outline takes shape against the sea.

I'm going to have to breathe.

Soon, I'm going to have to breathe.

His own breaths come ragged. He is tall, slender even. For a second, I recall the armed officers again. It's the burly ones that stick in my mind. I wonder if I could overwhelm a skinny one.

I wish he'd move.

I need to breathe, and unless he moves, he'll hear me. And then…

The stories of the highwaymen worm their way into my mind. The robbing and the violence, the unspeakable evil they do to girls…

Don't be silly, Janet; this is a servant of the law.

But I've just been part of the mob that drove him out.

I'm going to have to...

To my horror, when I do open my mouth to breathe, it produces a loud gasp.

That's it, I'm done for.

'Hoi! Is there someone there?'

It's in the Gaelic, and not as deep as I expected, but he must be crazy if he expects me to answer. I force myself not to move. He takes a slow step towards me.

Should I run?

I can see his outline, bigger as it approaches. He can't possibly see where I am exactly.

If I hit him in the face and then took off, I might have a chance...

But then something unexpected: a whisper.

'Janet?'

Now that does get my attention.

'Hector?'

I stumble out of the rocky shadows and actually hug a Top-House Mackay.

As soon as I realise what I'm doing I jump back. 'What on earth are you doing here?'

'Following you! Not that you've made it easy. I saw that Angus was injured and you heading down the road. And when I asked Father if I could go to make sure you were safe, he wanted me to check on Peggy and Mother. So I ran. As I got closer I heard your steps, or at least I hoped it was you. And I knew there was *someone* there, hiding by the rocks, but I imagined one of the soldiers, ready to slit my throat...' He trails off.

Hector Mackay from the Top House was as terrified as I was.

A giggle rises deep in my stomach, rumbles up through my throat and then I can't keep it in anymore, laughing out all my relief. Hector joins in but I wouldn't have cared if he hadn't. Together, we resume a brisk walk back to Ceannabeinne.

Hector is full of talk. 'That was quite something, wasn't it? I don't think our men meant to start a fire though. I heard one of the officers knocked a torch out of someone's hand inside the inn. I was in there with Angus, but I didn't see for myself. Seems likely though. Just as well people came with water straight away. It wasn't really the innkeeper's fault—he has to make a living, I suppose. Don't you think so, Janet?'

I say 'aye' and 'really' and *'èist!'* and things like that, content to let him talk because I have never been so glad of company in my life. Walking like that, side by side in the dark, the road propels us towards home. Soon, we are carefully picking our way down the slope into Ceannabeinne.

How can this path be so easy to run up and down in the day? Take away the light and it's treacherous. I nearly fall twice and Hector walks me all the way down to my home before retracing his steps up to the Top House. I expected Granna to have company—maybe Margaret Munro. Most of our neighbours were at Durine, I suppose. Except the two women in the hill cave. I plan to go up to see the Seamstress and Isabella after church tomorrow, if I'm spared.

Granna, however, is kneeling alone between the hearth and her box bed while the dying fire warms her back. She's wrapped in a shawl, too.

It must be the chill of loneliness. I feel it too—and shiver.

'Granna.' I speak softly, not wanting to startle her, but her Gaelic prayer flows and I stand back to listen. It's simply the natural language to pray in, even though the Reverend Findlater is clever enough to pray in English, too.

Surely the good Lord prefers the Gaelic. It's the language of the land, and He made the land, didn't He?

'Granna, I'm back,' I say a little louder, and this time she hears me. She finishes her prayers, with a "*Thy name be praised*" and rises with difficulty.

'What's the news, Janet?'

'I came to check on you and to fetch the mare. There was a riot, Granna, though Hugh spoke well and the Reverend pleaded with the Dornoch men. But they wouldn't listen; they wouldn't listen at all.'

Granna motions for me to sit by the hearth and I sink down gratefully. She lowers another cut of peat onto the feeble fire and it sends a billow of smoke upwards to the roof before igniting in rejuvenated flames.

'They said we had to leave tomorrow. On the Sabbath.'

Granna winces at that, but doesn't interrupt.

'...so Hugh and the Reverend tried again, but...' my voice fades.

There is too much too explain, too many things to describe. Thankfully, Granna seems to understand and nods.

'Mother and Father are fine, but Angus is injured. It's a cut on his leg, but it's deep. We need to get him home and see to the wound properly.'

Granna looks alarmed. 'Then lose no time, lass. Take the mare.'

The last thing I want to do is go back out there, into the dark and the cold. It's made a lot easier by Hector appearing, already leading the mare by the reins. His mother has come with him to fetch Granna to the Top House, and I'm truly grateful.

Hector stands up so straight he looks almost like a man. 'I thought I'd come back with you, Janet. For safety.'

'Two young ones like you two? Some safety that is,' Granna snorts, but I can tell she is glad of Hector's offer, and so am I.

Standing on the dry stone dyke around our garden courtyard, we jump on the horse's bare back and with a gentle kick, we're off.

Chapter Twenty-Two

The Sabbath

Through the narrow window, the sunrise sheds little light on our weary faces. Mother hasn't even gone to bed, giving her space in the box bed to Angus, who normally sleeps on the floor beside the hearth like me.

She wipes his forehead with a damp cloth and feeds him sips of water with a little whisky for the pain. Angus is doing his best to bear it like a man.

'Think of the scar you're going to have. You can pass yourself off as a soldier, injured in battle. That'll impress the girls!' I joke, reaching for the pail to fetch water for the brew.

However, my efforts to cheer up my brother fail to find approval. Angus just grimaces and Granna gives me the *'it's the Sabbath'* stare. Even on the short walk to the spring, I fancy seeing soldiers behind every rock and shrub.

But Catherine looks excited when she joins me to fetch

water for her own family.

'They're gone; truly gone. It seems that the Procurator Fiscal didn't even stop at Rispond, except to wait for the constables who were spread out all over the landscape. It's almost comical when you think of these men, hiding behind the corn stooks, isn't it, Janet?'

'How do you know they're gone?' The water trickles into my bucket. *Sweet music of morning. But how long?*

'Mary said so. Someone must have followed them.'

That's how things work in Ceannabeinne. We know things because we talk.

'See you in church.'

'Yes.'

Both of us are too tired for chit-chat.

An hour later, everyone in the village who can walk keeps a watchful eye on the hillside and the beaches while going to seek the help of the Lord in our time of need.

It's not a silent procession, though. Father talks in a low voice, only to us.

'The best we can hope for is time. If only we could get in the harvest. Make plans, sell what we don't need... Don't look so worried, lass. Angus will be fine.'

Mother nods, but her face is still tense.

So, it seems that Father is already moving on in his mind; concerned, but determined, too. Mother looks older this morning, and even her voice sounds like that of an aged woman. 'But Johnnie, don't you think they'll move us by force? Since they've made such a show of threatening us?'

Father stares into the distance, stops to help Granna over a particularly stony bit in the road, and answers after some thought.

'You're right, it would be a humiliation for them. One more humiliation. But let's have faith. Take in the harvest; sell what we can. Plan ahead; write to a few people. Others have had to cope with this before... and worse.' He takes a sidelong glance at Granna. 'Let's try to have faith.'

We reach the church, but there are only standing spaces left. I lead Granna to the front, and as usual, someone realises she needs the space in the pew more than they do. This time, it's a young woman from Sangobeg whose name I don't remember, but I give her a grateful smile anyway.

It's sheltered in here, with the glass panes to keep out the worst of the wind. I look around me and feel the bond of God's people, united in language and heart and fate.

The Precentor begins in steady notes, and the twenty-third psalm reverberates through the building in ornate patterns, as if voices danced, together and apart, following and leading as we take out the line: *God being our shepherd and we'll not want, even though we walk in the valley of the shadow of death.* As we sing in four, even five harmonies, the roof seems to lift and I am at peace for a moment.

Whatever happens.

Ceannabeinne, 1814: *The Golden Sand*

The cart pulled to a stop as the wide expanse of golden sand came into view. 'This is it, there beyond the bay.'

Anna looked across, squinting against the setting sun. ''Tis beautiful, right enough, John. Stony though.'

'We're lucky, Anna. Let's not be ungrateful for what the Lord has provided.'

John was right of course, Anna knew it.

'So we ask for shelter and then...'

'Begin building, what else?' Her husband smiled. A tense smile, but a smile all the same.

Their toddler leaned forward and pointed, giggling.

'He is looking at that big stone yonder, John. How do you think it got there?'

John's eyes followed his son's stubby pointing finger. 'Right up to the top of the hill? Couldn't tell you; such a big boulder.

Magic?'

Anna laughed, taking in the darkening sea below, terns hovering above the water in the evening light, darting in with melodic splashes and hovering again.

Ceannabeinne. The very word sounded alien to her.

She would need to think of it as home now.

Home.

*

Dinner is always simple on the Sabbath. I eat a bite before setting off up the hill to see Isabella and the Seamstress with the rest of the fish, bread and cheese. A jug of milk narrowly fits into the basket. Mother sighs.

'Make sure you keep it upright. And come straight back, Janet, mind that.' With this, she gives me one of Angus's woollen jerkins and nods for me to go.

Clambering over the rocks isn't easy with the hamper and I wonder how the two women managed with everything they would need. It all seems a lifetime ago: Isabella holding the knife to Mr Campbell's throat, that day I chased into the village. His startled horse, the knife, the stones—even the ferryman at Port Chamuil who told me about his own plight. What'll become of the ferry route, I wonder. Will there be no more ferries across Loch Eriboll at all? Or will the Master Anderson build a new pier, somewhere else? Who can tell?

An eagle flies overhead, disappearing into the clouds by Ben Hope. Following its path, I stumble and a little of the milk spills, but no matter. I can't fret over small things when all the big questions are pressing in on me.

If I could speak to the eagle, I know what I'd say: *I envy you and your eyrie, high on the Ben.*

*No-one's threatening to burn down **your** home. No-one can throw **you** off the land you call home.*

And if they try, you simply fly away.

Simply fly away.

It's these fanciful and wasted thoughts which occupy me until I reach the mouth of the cave.

I haven't been here for some time. There is a washing line, strung between two protruding rocks. Empty, of course— it is the Sabbath after all. A fire is kindled by the entrance to the cave, but the smoke still goes into the cavern, and there's no thatch through which it can escape. No wonder Isabella is coughing so hard in there. A candle burns beside the simple straw mattress on which she is laid out.

It's the middle of the day. Why is she in bed?

'Hello!' I shout, and the Seamstress answers from a little way off. I wait politely. She may be relieving herself or doing some washing, though it's the Sabbath and she shouldn't.

'Janet. Thank goodness.' There's genuine joy in her face. It's funny; in the village she barely spoke to me, but she seems so grateful for company now.

'Why is Isabella sleeping?'

The Seamstress hesitates. 'She is old, Janet; she is weak.'

I don't know what to say to that.

The Seamstress, however, seems eager to talk. 'So, tell me about the service at church. Did the Reverend say anything about what might happen? And how is Angus's leg—young William was here earlier; he told me.'

'Well, after the service, the Reverend said that he's written to the Duke of Sutherland and asked him to intervene. The newspapers are changing the way they are reporting on us up here and the Duke is bound to get involved now, for good or for ill; at least that's what the Reverend thinks.'

The Seamstress nods thoughtfully. I brace myself for an unwanted answer, but I have to ask all the same. Two questions. Two dreaded outcomes.

'Do you really think we'll have to leave?'

In the village, it's the one obvious thing to ask, and the one thing no-one mentions. Up here, in the dull confinement of the cave, it seems easier to say it.

'I'm afraid I do, lass. I can't see any way around it now.

But I'm hopeful, too—hopeful that the Lord will still have a purpose for us all.' Her round face is thinner now, but she smiles a sad smile.

I stare at the drips of water running down the stony wall of the cave.

'Wherever that may be,' she concludes.

My second question isn't long in coming, but I make sure it's in a whisper: 'And do you think Isabella is going to die?'

Here, the Seamstress resumes her brisk manner, rising immediately and checking the motionless bundle that is Isabella, tucked into the warmest corner of the cavern.

She returns and whispers, but looks no less industrious for it. 'Janet, the soul is attached to the body by a mere thread that can sever at any moment. Isabella is weak. *You* may topple off a cliff, *I* might catch a fever and die, Isabella may go before us both—or she may not. Don't attempt to predict the ways of the Lord.'

Isabella gives a moan and stirs in the smoky darkness.

Time to go. I wonder if our men know how bad things truly are.

I'm not fooled—the Seamstress is torn between her worry for Isabella and her fear of reprisals. I wonder how many times she has wished she'd never touched the knife, never addressed Sheriff Officer Campbell; just carried on cutting the bright printed cotton for the next Top-House dress. She *needs* all of us now.

It takes almost half the village to climb the hill that evening and fetch everything the women were using in the cave. We carefully retrace the path with their precious cargo: blankets, bundles of kindling, food parcels, clothes, cooking pots, two straw mattresses, and the bible the Seamstress's husband left behind, before setting off on the fishing trip that would claim his life. Hugh walks ahead and steadies the Seamstress along the narrow path, her figure a little less stout than I remember.

Father is carrying Isabella, mumbling into his unruly beard every time she shifts and knocks him off balance. All talking has long ceased and the curtains of darkness are drawing across the eastern sky once more. Another night.

Another escape.

We are exhausted by the time we reach the village at sundown. Mary's boys are standing guard, but there is no sign of our supposed Sabbath eviction. The Schoolmaster, however, shoots out of the whitewashed building to confront us as soon as we reach the schoolhouse.

'So it is true. Not only rioting and violence, not only disobedience and defiance—no! Now you are flouting the laws of God himself! The Sabbath calls for rest and worship, not household removals and hill walks. I'm ashamed of you!'

I glance at Isabella, but her eyes are closed and her body limp.

Hugh steps forward. 'You'd do well not to judge, Schoolmaster; you'd do well not to judge.'

None of us even give the Schoolmaster another glance; instead we march past him with the women's goods and ignore his shaking of the head as he calls us all the children of the devil. I'm one of the last to move past him, and I simply can't help myself:

'Doesn't love cover a multitude of sins? Where is your love, Schoolmaster?'

And I know that the beating tomorrow will be fierce and personal, but it's worth it—just to see his outraged pride.

CHAPTER TWENTY-THREE

Durine Square

THREE DAYS LATER, WE WALK TO THE CHURCH, AHEAD OF THE CART carrying Isabella's body. I know what I am supposed to do. Respectful silence and graceful composure; that's what is expected of me. But when the Reverend Findlater begins preaching about the heavenly home where Isabella can enjoy eternal rest, I'm not the only one who loses control.

For the first time in all of this, I cry properly. For the way things worked out; for my own part in it. For Granna and Isabella and the Seamstress, for Margaret Munro who everyone expects to enter eternity next, and for the future in a Rispond Estate without fishing or townships or songs or love. Nothing but sheep, only sheep.

And the tears begin to fall until Mother and Granna, and Angus on his wooden crutches, all embrace me together. Then sobs shake my body and the tears flood my face.

Another evening, another gathering in the church hall. I

love—and I hate—the way we do funerals.

I love the stories told by those who've known Isabella for longest. I love hearing about her as a young woman, betrothed to a soldier who never returned. I can't really picture her, inheriting the house by the beach from her parents who died within a year of each other, and earning a living from making and repairing fishing nets, always seeing justice done in the village. Lonely she may have been at times, but never alone, for the Lord was her constant companion, the Reverend says, and it comforts me to think of angels escorting her to heaven, attending her soul as she lay, back in her own cottage for her last night on this earth.

I hate the fact that I never knew any of this until she was gone. I wouldn't wish to end my life like her, feverish and on the run, no family, no children, no husband, no hope. But strangely, I also *do* want to end up like her, with courage and determination, the fearlessness of not being beholden to anyone but my own conscience.

And all the thinking exhausts me.

It's on our way back that we see the notices: one outside the church and another one on the post along the road, one on the schoolhouse wall and two pasted to the walls of the outhouses on the path into Ceannabeinne:

A Public Meeting will be held on Thursday at three o'clock at Durine Square. In attendance will be the Sheriff of Sutherland: Mr Lumsden, of Dornoch.

Representatives of all Rispond Estate townships MUST attend.

Between us, we manage to translate it word for word from the English, although I'm sure the Reverend would have done it quicker and better. Hugh nods thoughtfully and marches faster to catch up with Father.

'The Sheriff himself?' I hear Father ask. 'Is there any higher authority in Sutherland?'

'Only the Duke, and he is far away,' Hugh answers.

'Told you it isn't over, Janet,' says Angus. 'It'll not be over till we give in.'

'But a meeting so soon? Tomorrow. Do you think he'll be on his way already, Angus?'

My brother nods. 'The Sheriff will not delay longer than necessary.'

I slow my step so he can keep up and look at him. 'Are we really worth that? To bother the Sheriff of Sutherland himself?'

Angus sighs. 'A man, is a man, is a man. He'll boil his eggs in water like the rest of us, Janet.'

I can see my brother struggle with his crutches, but there's nothing I can do unless he lets me help him. Twice I open my mouth to ask if he'd like me to run ahead to fetch the mare, but he just clamps his teeth together as if to bite off the pain and I leave it be.

The following day passes in a haze of grief and grievance. No-one even credits the most important man in Sutherland with a glance when he rides past to Durine on his shiny black horse. I think it's the Master Anderson behind him in a carriage, but I can't be sure and I don't want to look too closely. Once they are past us, I glance up again. Another four uniformed men, their weapons gleaming in the sunlight.

Who are we fooling? No-one but ourselves.

'No despairing now, lass. He may have come to make peace.' Hugh tries hard to be cheerful on the way to the meeting, but I can tell that even he, the great Hugh Munro, is running out of courage. His forehead is furrowed with deep crevasses, like pitfalls of defeat. I say nothing.

Father—who is walking behind—puts his hand on Hugh's shoulder for a moment. Angus is riding the mare this time with Granna sitting sideways behind him and holding on around his waist.

Look at us.

The Ceannabeinne army.

What a joke.

And at that moment, the last remaining hope is evicted from my heart. We will be driven out. Maybe even before the night is out.

The mare slows as we approach the square in Durine. The weather is dreich, not a ray of sunshine for warmth now. There's a makeshift platform for the Sheriff to speak from, but I can't see him, nor can I see the Master Anderson, although some of the women already gathered say he went by earlier. It isn't long before the square is fuller than I have ever seen it. All of us: Ceannabeinne, Rispond, Port Chamuil, all the smallholdings in between, and it also appears that the whole of Durine, Smoo and Sangomore are here. I even recognise a family from the islands, although how they knew about the meeting at such short notice is beyond me.

Soon, a portly figure is ushered to the platform and climbs up awkwardly. The soldiers position themselves between him and us, hands on their hilts, but there is no appetite for violence today. I don't know *how* I know it, but I'm certain. We're just like the sheep which will replace us on the land: useful up to a point. Stupid, impulsive, dirty, powerless.

Fit for slaughter.

And the Reverend, supposedly the shepherd of our flock, isn't even here yet.

All of us stand back a little, so I get a good view of the Sheriff of Sutherland with his shiny hat and grey-black moustache. Beside him, is the now familiar face of the Superintendent. The Sheriff is older, no stranger to many rich dinners when you look at his shiny shirt straining against the waistband of his breeches. I look over my shoulder at the Seamstress and, as I suspected, she, too, looks mesmerised by the shiny velvet of his ceremonial jacket. Does he go to work in these garments every day? Or does he wear it to impress on us that they are the masters and we are the servants?

He stares out the whispers until silence settles like dusk.

'People of Rispond!' he yells, and I'm not the only one who jumps. Angus drops one of his crutches and has to lean on Father to keep his balance.

'Listen to this, in the Scotsman newspaper, only last week: *"Uncouth Highlanders Bent on Violence Once Again"*. Or The Times newspaper, all the way down in London: *"Riot and Disorder in Sutherland"*. And a little closer to home, from the Inverness Courier: *"Rebellion at Sutherland Estate—Villagers Defy King and Country—Serious Consequences Likely"*.

He waits, letting the headlines do their work, like leaving the knife in the wound before twisting it out. The waiting strikes fear and he must know it. Hugh is hanging his head. Across the crowd, the Schoolmaster smirks and I imagine a torturous corner of hell, reserved only for him.

'Face facts! You have defied the law and all its representatives. Beginning with this humble servant of the law before you...'

He gestures his lacy sleeve at a man in our midst. Right enough, it is Mr Campbell of Port Chamuil; not that I would have recognised him when he's dressed just like us. None of us can quite meet his eyes, but he, too, looks uncomfortable, being singled out.

The Sheriff continues: '...*inflicting horrific injuries, resulting in his leaving the Sheriff Service for good.*'

But Campbell shakes his head. His arms do look scarred, even from this distance I can see that. The Sheriff on the platform draws a breath to go on, but to all our surprise, the man Campbell speaks into the silence first.

'I was hurt, aye. But I left because I wanted no part in the Master Anderson's schemes anymore. I myself am losing my home.' One of the uniformed men takes a step towards him, and Campbell holds his hands out as if to say he's said what he came to say. *That took courage, to speak out like that*. Many look at him now in silent apology for the hurt we caused him.

As if no-one had interrupted, the Sheriff speaks on:

'Now, the end of all of this is inevitable. Master Anderson of Rispond holds the lease from the Duke, so he can do as he pleases. For the good of the estate, it has been decided to focus on sheep-farming, which necessitates the end of the townships. Of course, we are not without sympathy towards your plight. But what you must realise is that you have set yourself against the law. The law is against you. The press is against you. The British Empire and its educated public are against you. But it need not end this way.'

I understand now how this man achieved such a position of high authority. His voice rings out, not unlike a minister's, and none of us can help seeing reason. He can make a speech, make no mistake.

'It need not end this way because, even at this late stage, Master Anderson is willing to be merciful and not press charges against the perpetrators of the violence. Even in the face of provocation and defiance, he will show grace.'

Mercy and *grace* are not words which spring to mind when describing Anderson of Rispond, and Catherine who knows him best clearly agrees. Her face is incredulous. There is a hint of muttering: all of us are worried about our men. *No gallows? At what price?*

'The demand is clear. Leave your homes to be demolished and never come back. Settle elsewhere. Go to the cities if you want, and make a living there. There's plenty of honest labour to be had in the factories if you're willing to work hard. Or set out for the New World with its promise of wealth and adventure. In any case...'

He pauses to deliver the death blow, and even though I know it's coming, I still wince.

'...be gone by tomorrow night.'

There are shouts and groans. Granna sways and I hold on to her, with the Seamstress putting her arm round us both from the other side. But the Sheriff isn't finished. And this time he holds a card that none of us are expecting him to play.

His gleaming crooked teeth shine with victory as he concludes: 'The 53rd regiment of Scotland are already on standby. They will be here to deal with any... difficulty. Now, are there any questions?'

That was clever, really clever. He must realise that all of us are too stunned to protest, and his Gaelic translator is still speaking for the benefit of those who haven't enough English to make sense of it all.

The Sheriff walks to the edge of the platform. Out of the

shadows, the Master Anderson appears to shake hands with him. The soldiers' eyes are still on the crowd.

The whole 53rd Regiment of Scotland! The name is like a knife, carving dread into my heart. They would show no mercy. So many would die.

Of course I fear tomorrow. I fear the unknown. I fear the cities, I fear the New World.

But I am *terrified* of what a whole regiment of soldiers could do if *we* were the enemy.

Chapter Twenty-Four

The Duke's Seal

'Tomorrow it is.' Mother joins the Seamstress, Granna and me. Her voice is dead.

'I wonder if he has the authority to summon the Regiment at all,' says Hugh, slightly louder than is probably wise. The speech, and the meeting, is clearly over. Everywhere, people begin to talk, to cry. But nobody is pleading anymore. Faint hoof beats become louder. The Sheriff steps down from the platform. I see now that their horses are saddled and waiting. I don't blame him; not after what happened last time. He won't be intending to spend the night here in Durine. There is rain in the air and I'm sure the fires are already crackling in Anderson's Rispond grates to welcome his victorious visitors.

But the bewildered crowd scatters when the Reverend Findlater, agitated and out of breath, rides his sweat-drenched horse right into the middle of the square and up to the platform where the Sheriff is buttoning up his coat.

'Halt and delay!' he wheezes, waving a piece of paper. His horse rears and before I know what I'm doing, I've pushed my way through and snatched her dangling reins. I like his mare, and the poor man looks as if he might faint. I use my other hand to steady him as he dismounts. Faith. Hope. Love. Fragments of sermons spin in my head. *What is he doing?*

'It's done, Findlater. Leave it be,' the Master Anderson snaps, turning away, but the Reverend will not be silenced.

'I have a letter.' The Minister is shouting it between deep, ragged breaths.

'Well, Reverend, we are done here, if you don't mind. Unless your letter is from the Lord God himself, you'd do well not to meddle.' Anderson and the Sheriff laugh loudly, but I flinch at such ungodliness.

Reverend Findlater's voice rings clear now: 'What if the letter was from the Duke of Sutherland who owns all the land beneath your feet and ours—as far as your own home in Dornoch? Would you dismiss *him* so lightly?'

I hold my breath. *Could it be? If anyone could help us, surely the Duke can?*

'This letter bears the seal of the Duke of Sutherland himself,' Findlater continues. 'I wrote to him to beg his assistance in our hour of need. See for yourself!'

He clutches the letter to his chest as if someone might steal it while he clambers up the platform. Reluctantly, the Sheriff joins him.

'Do you, Mr Lumsden, Sheriff of Sutherland, acknowledge the seal of your Duke?'

The Sheriff mumbles something, but Findlater insists. 'Do you?'

'It is his seal, yes, but…'

'I'll read this letter in the hearing of everyone, as it concerns you all. I don't know what it says—I had to leave the seal intact to prove I haven't meddled with it. God is my witness. These are the words of the Duke of Sutherland.'

We are so quiet that I fancy I can actually hear the seal break. Then the Reverend begins, reading each sentence in English and translating into the Gaelic before the next.

'Dear Reverend Findlater,

Thank you for your letters pertaining to the proposed Rispond Estate reorganisation. As you will be aware, the nature of the lease held by Mr Anderson allows me no authority over the running of the estate until the lease returns to me. However, please use this letter as my personal plea to your master to suggest a compromise. Instead of forcing the tenants to leave before the winter, unable to bring in and sell the full harvest or to put their affairs in order and make plans for their future, may I ask that he consider giving tenants leave to stay until May of next year. This would be, I'm sure, an acceptable solution for all concerned. It also seems to me that the plight of the villagers has been misrepresented in the press—I have written to the papers concerned. I am confident that a more balanced view will be published within days.'

Still we stand, stumped by so many turns of events. The Sheriff looks as if he has swallowed sheep dung. Anderson's eyes are narrow and mean. But the Reverend isn't finished reading yet.

'I will, of course, exert all possible influence to ensure kind and compassionate treatment for all Rispond Estate tenants. When Sheriff Lumsden returns to Dornoch, he will find instructions to this effect from me.'

The transformation of Sheriff Lumsden is absolute. Less than half an hour ago, he was the charismatic, rousing speaker of authority. Now he is a scolded schoolboy. Anderson swears loudly. 'Let's go, Sheriff Lumsden. *I* hold the lease. It makes no difference!'

But the Sheriff doesn't move; he only looks at the letter the Reverend holds out before him. At long last, he speaks, but his powerful voice has become shrill and hoarse.

'The Duke is a man of principle and influence, a man who has the ear of the King himself.' He shoots a look of apology at Anderson who spits on the ground and turns away in disgust.

'Anderson is your master, your tacksman. Of course, he must be obeyed. But since the Duke himself has requested the delay… It would seem prudent, in the light of today's events, to grant that delay.'

The Sheriff is clearly not used to having to contradict himself within thirty minutes. It's like the whole assembled crowd can't breathe, strangled by this new, unexpected hope. He seems to be suggesting that, maybe… maybe…

I wish he'd speak; let us know one way or the other. And then he raises his voice.

'As Sheriff for Sutherland, I recommend that the time of eviction be set for next spring: May 1842. In return for this undeserved kindness in the face of such barbaric provocation, you will make plans for your future and leave willingly. There will be no more unrest or hostility. Master Anderson?'

All eyes are on Anderson now, even though he has no choice—not really. His mouth is a tense line. He reaches for the reins of his horse.

The cheering is still going on when the procession of

important officials disappears towards the east. Mother and Granna are locked in a sort of jumping embrace which surely is unbecoming for someone of Granna's age, but all of us just laugh. The relief rolls in with the breakers, soaking into us like salt water into sand. By the end of the night, I've lost count of the amount of people I have hugged or shaken hands with. Hector actually grabs me and swings me once all around before he runs home to tell Margaret Munro the news.

'It's so strange,' I say to Catherine and Wee Donald, walking beside me on the way home. 'It's not like we won. We're being turned out after all, but still we celebrate and sing.'

Catherine nods. 'And Isabella not here to see our last winter together.'

Wee Donald wriggles in between us and holds each of our hands, squeezing hard.

'But *we* are t-together. Catherine, J-Janet and Wee Donald.'

'For one more winter, yes,' I agree. 'And that's good enough for me!' Even though the way is only lit by the torch Angus is holding, I can't help racing ahead; running out the relief, and Wee Donald and Catherine chase me all the way to the schoolhouse bend. Back in the longhouse, I light a candle and do battle with the damp peat until a small fire begins to warm and light the stony darkness.

Angus hobbles in after seeing to the mare. He, too, is humming.

'I do wonder how conversation is flowing in Rispond right now,' he says. 'I wouldn't be surprised if Anderson never spoke to the Sheriff again. He looked murderous enough for a massacre.'

'He'll get over it,' says Father who has come in beside me, smelling of cattle and the land. 'There's nothing else he can do now.'

'I was speaking to Findlater's maid earlier,' Mother adds. 'She said the Reverend stayed at the manse instead of coming to the meeting, waiting and praying that a response would come before it was too late. And then the messenger came with the letter. A miracle, no doubt about that.'

Granna is on the box bed. All of us sit quietly, and I would be willing to bet the whole harvest that each of us is uttering a heart-prayer, thanking the good Lord for one more winter.

Soon after, I lie in the dark beside the dying flames of the hearth, staring up at the roof thatch that could have gone up in flames tomorrow.

185

But it is *not* going to go up in flames tomorrow.

It'll bow and drip under ice and snow; it'll sing with the wind and rustle with mice, it'll filter our peat smoke into the sky. It'll bend and shiver with the roar of the sea.

One more winter.

And I'm a little surprised:

It *is* good enough for me.

CHAPTER TWENTY-FIVE

The Leaving Gift

THEY ARE COMING. THERE ARE FOURTEEN MEN, NO, WAIT, seventeen, all marching towards us, rolling up their sleeves to turn homes into rubble, houses into scattered stones.

Father must read my mind. 'They have their orders, Janet. Come on.'

We wrap the blanket around Granna before she takes the wobbly seat on the cart beside Mother. We are the last ones. Everybody else is already gone.

I should be sad, I suppose. Heartbroken even—but maybe a heart cracks a wee bit at a time.

Like the time in January when we finally laid Margaret Munro to rest.

Like two weeks ago when Wee Donald and Catherine left for Glasgow.

Like the day before yesterday when the Top House Mackays set fire to their own roof and Hector, Mr Mackay, Father and Angus pushed the walls in themselves because the Top House family couldn't bear their lovely home being destroyed by Anderson's men. Peggy even let me put my arm round her shoulder as she wept. I wonder if we will be anywhere near them in Canada.

Like Hugh's departure, just up the road to Durine so he could be near to Margaret's grave.

A wee bit at a time.

I do smile a little at the memory of the Schoolmaster. I don't know what he expected? Maybe he thought he was going to live out his days in comfort. Teaching the children of the shepherds, perhaps?

When an officer told him his house would be required for shepherd accommodation, he whined like an old woman. Somewhere Aberdeen way, he went. And good riddance.

Someone had to stay till the end, I suppose. Not sure why; but it seemed right. As the eviction mob floods down the hill to begin their dirty work on Isabella's beach cottage, there is nothing left to hold us here. Nothing and no-one.

We stop by the manse. Father promises he'll stay in touch and the Reverend prays for us before we set off. I stay in the cart with Granna. I feel that if I touch the land again, my foot will remain glued right here where I belong.

Hugh waves from his brother-in law's house by the shore. He doesn't come up to the road and we do not go down.

When I look back, I see the columns of smoke from Ceannabeinne way. Fourteen houses. Fourteen homes. In time, the smoke from them all mingles together and climbs high—until the wind blows it where it wishes.

It's not until the end of the day, when we stop at the inn at Rhiconich, that we open the leaving gift from the Reverend. It's a book about Canada, beautifully illustrated and a real treasure.

'Wait there, lass.' Granna reaches past me and runs her finger over a picture near the front. 'Let me see it closely, Janet.' I pass the book to her and take the candle off the table to hold it right above the page.

'Read what it says. Please, lass.'

The picture looks a bit boring to me, only landscape. Trees, water, hills... I clear my throat and translate the English caption into the Gaelic as best as I can.

'Canadian vegetation is varied and rich, but conifer trees are arguably the most common. The balsam fir grows in abundance in Eastern Canada.'

She smiles at me, reaches into her pocket, unfolds a

small, worn white handkerchief and shows me. The remains of the sprig of fir tree, all those months ago. Dried out and crumbling, but here it is, in her hand, travelling with us to Glasgow, God-willing then on to Canada and goodness knows where next…

Canada is full of fir trees.

'Fir for luck,' she whispers.

Her bony fingers find mine in the strange room, across a stranger's table. The squeeze of her hand takes me back to the longhouse, to the village, to the land. I take a deep, deep breath: home is right here, in the smallest of gestures.

'Fir for luck,' she repeats, wrapping the sprig up once more and sliding it between the pages of the book.

'You'll see, Janet. You'll see…'

The End

Author's Note

I'm a writer. If I sense a story, my ears prick up.

So when I came across the crumbling ruins of Ceannabeinne on holiday in Sutherland in 2013, I couldn't believe my luck! There it was, ready-made and there for the taking: the most incredible tale of local defiance; courage, drama, the haves and the have-nots. A textbook tale with a crisis, plenty of conflict and a near-miraculous resolution. A villain and a whole village of heroes.

The *what-ifs* came first: *What if* the first person to spot the officer with the writ was a girl? *What if* her quick reaction made all the difference? *What if* she and her friends were at the heart of it all? Words began to dance in my mind and I knew I was going to write about this forsaken place, with its golden beach dissolving into glittering surf, into sea and sky. The emptiness had a beauty, but it also had a story. And what a story!

I looked into it. No, it hadn't been written about in fiction before, certainly not for children. In fact, most children's books about the Highland Clearances had been published four decades ago and focused on Strathnaver and Patrick Sellar. I realised I'd have to make clear that the Clearances happened over several decades. This is where the idea of Granna's tale and the flashbacks came from. After all, it was highly likely that some survivors of the violent Sellar years had re-settled on the coast.

So yes—a lot of *Fir for Luck* actually happened. The women and children really had to face the officer alone, as the men were away thatch-cutting. And they did indeed overwhelm him and force him to burn the writ. Many of the details in the story are also historically documented: the shouts for help from the top of the hill; the trusty party; the Mackintosh coat; rocks being hurled at the official from Dornoch; and even the letter from the Duke and the newspaper coverage. As for Anderson, the Superintendent, Patrick Sellar, and the Reverend Findlater—these men all really existed.

The villagers, however, are fictional characters based on real households. I found a list of the families who lived at Ceannabeinne at the time and mixed up the names to create new combinations. My villagers' jobs are authentic and most of them worked for Anderson. Incidentally, the top house ruin really did have a flagstone floor and gable-end chimneys; clearly the most affluent family in the village resided there. The plot device of the Top-House Mackays and their obsession with status was born.

So if you are lucky enough to travel to Sutherland, do look out for the Big Boulder beside the road opposite the schoolhouse (now holiday accommodation). Take the Ceannabeinne Trail and walk past the Top House and across the burn. Visit the Strathnaver Museum where I learned about the fir sprig, wound into the hearth chain for luck, and a million other details besides. Look down onto the golden sand and hear 'the waves in the distance roll in like a heartbeat, steady and strong'.

Feel it all come alive for you—as it did for me.

Barbara

Barbara Henderson
Inverness, September 2016

Glossary

Ben - mountain, often short for Ben Hope

bent - a reedy grass

Bent Day - a set day on which men cut new thatch for their village

bere - a kind of grain

beremeal - ground-up bere, a kind of flour

braw - grand, fine

byre - the part of the longhouse reserved for the animals

cairn - a mound of rough stones, usually built as a memorial or landmark

ceilidh - a social gathering with music

chanter - practice bagpipe, similar to a recorder

dour - gloomy, stern

dreich - bleak, dreary (often used to describe weather)

Duke - nobleman landowner, the highest rank below the king or queen

éist! - (Gaelic) gosh!

eviction - forcing someone out of a rented property (or off rented land)

Factor - someone put in charge of managing an estate

feasgar math - (Gaelic) good day

footman - a servant whose duties include serving meals

haar - a dense sea fog

hearth - the fireplace inside the house

heath - moorland covered in low shrubs like heathers

lochan - small inland loch/lake

machair - grassy coastline

madainn mhath - (Gaelic) good morning

party - a group of people with a common purpose

precentor - the man who leads psalm-singing at church

Procurator Fiscal - a powerful official who makes sure that criminals are brought to justice

regiment - a military unit, with often as many as a thousand soldiers

runrig - a traditional communal farming system based on strips of land

Sabbath - Sunday

seamstress - a woman who sews for a living

special constable - a person trained as a police officer for particular occasions

sheriff - highest-ranking legal official

sheriff officer - an officer who serves legal documents and enforces court orders

sheriff superintendent - a promoted post in the sheriff service

tacksman - land-holder of medium status, tends to lease the land from the owner

tawse - a leather strap / belt used by schoolmasters to discipline pupils

tenant - person who occupies land or property rented from a landlord

thatch - dry straw or grass used to cover a roof

trusty party - a group of hired fighters

writ - an official document containing a legal command

Acknowledgements

Thanks to...

Anne and Helen of Cranachan, for believing in this book and loving the story as much as I do—I'm hugely grateful. Graham Bruce, local historian, who agreed to check my manuscript for historical accuracy—a huge weight off my mind! Also to Nicola Poole for generously allowing me to use her wonderful illustration. My incredible pal Sandra McGowan for being *Fir for Luck's* first reader and my most unwavering supporter—she always believed it would happen one day! My Mum, my sisters Margund and Ricarda, and my Dad, who was around long enough to see the beginnings of some writing success. Rachel and Martin Hamilton—miss you guys a lot!

My fantastic SCBWI critique group for their honest feedback on the manuscript and writerly moral support through the ups and the downs—you guys get it. The children's writer Heather Dyer and Peter Urpeth of Emergents for their general comments on my writing and seeing ways of making it better. Cas Meadowfield for being the first follower on my blog whom I didn't actually know—you made me feel like I had something worth saying! Robert Taylor who goes the extra lightyear every time. Gerry and Ross Wiseman for help with the website and the book trailer. Strathnaver Museum—nothing was too much trouble. The teachers and pupils of Crown Primary for their enthusiasm and feedback.

And all of you who have helped and cheered me on my writerly ride, again and again. I can't thank you enough and I'm privileged to know you: my friends, my colleagues, my church.

That kid who came up to me in the street and told me he loved my book—you made me cry and you don't even know it—thank you!

Most of all, Rob—for encouraging me to teach part-time so I could write. For loving me enough to just get on with all the things I wasn't doing while I was writing! For believing in me enough to rush out during my meeting with the publishers to get champagne and flowers, just in case it worked out. For understanding how important this is to me.

And my amazing kids, Carla, Isla and Duncan who have that fantastic gift: they know how to be truly happy for someone else. I love you all. God really has been good to me.

'Grateful' doesn't even begin to cover it!

About the Author

Barbara was born in Germany in 1971, but has spent all of her adult life in Scotland, roaming from Edinburgh University (where she did an English degree) to Fife (for her first teaching job) to Inverness, London, Stonehaven and back to Inverness again. She now splits her time between teaching and writing.

She lives with her husband Rob, two teenage daughters and younger son. She loves Scotland's wild places, puppetry, folk music, crumbling buildings and old books—you know the ones, with the scent of stories.

Barbara was shortlisted for the Kelpies Prize in 2013, and writes short stories and drama, as well as fiction for children. Find out more about Barbara on her website barbarahenderson.co.uk.

Fir for Luck is her first published novel. She is delighted that this story, which began in her imagination and—let's be honest—consumed her mind for a time, is now going to connect with readers.

Her hope is that it might now spark their own imaginations, and perhaps consume their minds for a time.

And that, maybe, they will feel a little richer for it.

Yesteryear Series

Punch
by Barbara Henderson

Runaway Phin's journey across Victorian Scotland with an escaped prisoner and a dancing bear.

Charlie's Promise
by Annemarie Allan

A frightened refugee arrives in Scotland on the brink of WW2 and needs Charlie's help.

The Beast on the Broch
by John K. Fulton

Scotland, 799 AD. Talorca befriends a strange Pictish beast; together, they fight off Viking raiders.

The Revenge of Tirpitz
by M. L. Sloan

The thrilling WW2 story of a boy's role in the sinking of the warship Tirpitz.

Thank You for Reading

As we say at Cranachan,
'the proof of the pudding is in the reading'
and we hope that you enjoyed *Fir for Luck*.

Please tell all your friends and tweet us with your
#firforluck feedback, or better still, write an online review
to help spread the word!

We only publish books which excite and inspire us, so
if you'd like to experience other unique and
thought-provoking books, please visit our website:

cranachanpublishing.co.uk

and follow us
@cranachanbooks
for news of our forthcoming titles.

cranachan